Quests for Love

Novella by Roger Juchau

BONNIE

Warm spring mornings at the plant nursery never fail to raise Bonnie's spirits even when manoeuvring heavy seedling trays around the display benches. Dead seedlings and deformed punnets do not unsettle her buoyancy. The odd tray spill by her lax assistant does not disrupt her mood. And the ever circulating and bossy supervisor is not a concern when the sun is on her back.

Bonnie enjoys her work. There is something uplifting about a work place which offers surrounds in which life and renewal are symbolised in plant growth and flourish. Seasons do not detract. There is new life all year round. Plants of all dimensions form an exotic panorama of vigour in the tableau of shrubs, trees, palms, ferns, potted blooms, and herbs. Their endless variety of foliage offers a rich encounter of shapes and beauty. The sun adds a further pulse to nursery life as plants respond to its beckoning. Bonnie is greeted by this floral profusion when entering her foliage heaven.

Regular shoppers sense a special cordiality in their dealings with Bonnie, who graciously handles questions on plants, soils, pesticides, and fertilizers. Aiding her authority and assuredness is her quaint accent which is attributed to her late mother who came from Nova Scotia. Repetitive queries on plant cultivation never irritate her. Colleagues are amazed at her patience when serving 'the ethnics' as termed by her assistant. Their language struggles and multi-hued accents always find a receptive Bonnie. Even amongst the abrupt of Arabia, the earnest of the Orient, the know-alls of the Mediterranean and the quizzical of the Americas do not undermine her composure.

Bonnie is part of a team working nine-day fortnights at the garden centre. It is both a therapeutic and congenial haven from home which, since her divorce, has prevented her from feeling adrift. When not at work, her mid-twenties data analyst son, Jason, rarely emerges from his bedroom and adds little to home life.

The gossip, the ribaldry and the happenings of co-workers liven her day and carry her through the dark periods of solitude. Customer engagement and interactions often propel her to reflect about their lives and habits. And when the odd compliment or friendly gesture crosses her bow, the 51-year-old especially feels the absence and yearning that her divorcee-years have produced.

Surprising her is the amount of time spent when imagining the life and fortunes of frequent shoppers. She notes that men are in the minority on most days. Women dominate and come from a cross section of all ages. Young mums with nippers in tow, the middle-aged with their written lists of plants to buy, the elderly with weathered handbags and the occasional quarter-life crisis singles, largely comprise this cavalcade of shoppers. The politeness propensity of buyers is skewed. The young especially seem to ignore the courtesy lexicon - please, excuse me, and thank you - all now belonging to an older generation.

The older female regulars entering her horticultural world seem to be seeking diversion from their normal routines as well as enriching their domestic plant life. They always like a chat, especially the largely middle-aged cultivators temporarily visiting Bonnie's floral haven. Most are generally dressed well and there is evidence of recent salon visits. Bonnie has her favourites including Lee, a petite

Vietnamese, Phyllis of Greek descent, and Stella a confident ex- kiwi. Their regular visits enable Bonnie to build a profile of their horticultural tastes as well an impression of lives spent away from botanical pursuits.

Lee, a long-time resident in Australia, has adult children and a husband, who is skilled in gardening- avoidance, preferring to socialise in his leisure time. Lee has her bubbly and cheerful moments but there are times she appears to be burdened with a heavy sadness. Phyllis, affable and assured, is a second-generation Greek possessing deep knowledge of matters horticultural, and is quick to pass on her plant wisdom if requested. Her stoutness does not appear to inhibit her love to cultivate and surprises with accounts of her numerous gardening projects. There is a husband who remains outside Phyllis's conversational orbit.

Stella especially intrigues. Bonnie's unearthing has revealed that Stella, a 52-year-old single parent, is unsettled with her professional job and gardening is one of her rare pleasures. Stella has a 28-year-old daughter, Clare, living at home, who, despite many opportunities, has not tied the conjugal knot.

The slim, winsome Stella has a subdued coquettishness which enchants. Bonnie is perplexed by her reaction to Stella - how is it that she feels captivated or drawn to this seedling-fancier. Sauntering with Stella among the seedling trays gives an opportunity to converse and to enter her private world.

Days at work remove Bonnie from the overhang from her divorce which, despite the lapse of time, still brings sadness. Failed efforts to avoid divorce, the continued downward drift of a caring relationship, aided by a reducing libido, steered her marriage to the inevitable divide. Close friendships since the divorce have not formed, even among work mates. Her customers provide a means to connect and enliven her emotional life. A friendship with Stella could offer a possible chance to enter a world where feelings and confidences are shared and a sense of belonging regained.

Bonnie has pondered how she might approach Stella about a social get together without signalling an over keenness to associate. Her reading about the plight of middle-aged single women developing new friendships has not boosted her confidence, despite media commentators observing that mature women form friendships more easily than men of similar vintage. Normally confident in social contexts, the approach to Stella has her mildly unnerved. But such apprehension was quickly set aside when Stella suggested that they have coffee together in Bonnie's lunch hour.

Waking early on the coffee day, Bonnie was surprised by the tingling apprehension the coffee date produced. After showering and putting on her work outfit she modified her usual make up by applying a new shade of eye liner which, she believed, complimented her long ash-blonde hair. She wondered whether the logoed, high-collared, polo work shirt was getting too tight and notes to request a larger size. Aware of her fulsomeness Bonnie always lets her shirt remain untucked over her work slacks. As a final touch, Bonnie tied a colourful ribbon on her plait which sits her over left shoulder. Despite the unflattering outfit, a check in the hall mirror gives Bonnie confidence that her appearance does not cancel out her solid beauty, as described by her mum.

The garden centre coffee shop, arrayed with potted palms and hanging baskets, falls victim to the agricultural scents emanating from bags of horticultural supplements stored nearby. Its glass enclosure mimicking a classic conservatory, fails to deaden the sounds of chattering patrons. Lunch hour presents the usual crush of Friday plant seekers. They include several elderly grandparents corralling their baby-sit assignments, who are generating a noisy state of upheaval drawing annoyed looks from the youthful, acned baristas. Bonnie secures a table at the rear of the shop which, despite the gabble of Neapolitan ladies at an adjoining table, offers a nook of relative privacy and quietness.

A seated Bonnie spies Stella appearing at the entrance. What startled Bonnie is her striking coral-coloured dress and matching sparkling elongated earrings. Her normal mid-cut brown hair seemed shortened and, from a distance, looks spikey. Their greeting is followed by a chat about the glorious Spring they are enjoying and how their respective adult charges are faring. Stella outlines some changes planned for her garden and whether to replace lounge curtains with shutters. Bonnie has trouble mustering incidental conversation, finding herself mesmerized by the radiant latte drinker sitting opposite her. As Stella chats on Bonnie feels she is plummeting into some enrapture vortex as well as losing grasp of coffee chat protocols. Finally, as they depart, Stella mentions a forthcoming weekend open garden exhibition in the Blue Mountains and invites Bonnie to accompany her.

Concentrating on work that afternoon was hard. Bonnie wondered whether her acceptance to go to the exhibition was rash. No matter how much she tried to focus on the punnet sorting, the image of Stella, with her charm and grace, managed to distract. One of her regular customers commented that Bonnie seemed unusually preoccupied as she placed four rather than two punnets of Pansies in the customer's shopping trolley.

The invitation was still echoing through her mind on her drive home to her Ryde residence. The growing awfulness of her Ryde neighbourhood did not dampen her elation over the invitation. The creeping high-rise shabbiness, the scatter of unhoused garbage bins on the verges, the congested kerbside car parking, the epidemic of traffic signs and lights, the massacred trees freeing electricity wires and the soulless front gardens did not annoy her today. Arriving home even the smell of Jason's garlic-enhanced burnt evening meal wafting down the hallway did not irritate as she goes to the laundry to collect a load from the spin dryer.

Days seemed to fly since the invitation. She wondered if this was the start of breaking her companionship drought. Bonnie reviewed her wardrobe which had become a bit worn and outdated over the eleven years since divorce. She resolved to visit a local factory outlet to seek leisure wear to celebrate the trip away. She already made a booking to visit the hairdresser and, on a whim, she fixed an appointment to visit a 'Brows and Lashes' salon recommended by a younger work colleague.

A period before an important social occasion can bring apprehension and thoughts arise about whether it will unfold without disappointment. Bonnie tried to override these by focussing on work tasks. House chores, weeding the garden and tidying up shrubbery, all helped. Jason, sensing his mother's outburst of activity, did not question her household zeal yet suffered her usual riposte for his persistent neglect of sharing household chores and cleaning.

The email from Stella detailing the arrangements for the mountain trip elevated Bonnie's anxiety about whether a friendship would emerge. During her marriage, old friendships has been allowed to slip and not renewed. And work and post-divorce adjustments seemed to crowd out real opportunities to invest in activities to build friendships. She also had a real sense that her negative emotional outlook may have precluded any close relationship. For too long the fun out of life had eluded her and she doubted whether it was possible to restore. And the ever-present Jason did not help matters. His mood swings and intermittent boorishness sometimes took their toll on her emotional outlook.

Perhaps the advent of Stella might possibly allow Bonnie to pay more attention to her own welfare and Jason's welfare agendas would no longer be paramount. Jason, since adulthood, had not been concerned about Bonnie's outside ventures and welcomed the freedom of the house when she was away. He was unaffected by Bonnie's commitments and associations and rarely enquired about her life outside the home. Bonnie was not surprised when Jason made no comment about her trip except for a half-baked cynical comment about the bush flies encountered in mountain bushland.

Pondering relationships Bonnie thought about what it is about a friendship that contributes to well-being. Bonding, caring, sharing, companionship and buddy aspects are important. Deep down, at its core, it allows you to reach out to enjoy an honest, confidential interplay of emotions and views. Bonnie felt that her periods of despondency and joylessness might be attributed to not having a soul mate or two.

Bonnie reflected about Stella as she attended to her routines. It seemed that Stella's inbuilt charm was underpinned by a vigour in character and a disguised sensuality. Particularly impressive was her striking femineity, her radiant face and intelligent expression. Her lean body did not deny her a shapely chest and hips. Conversations revealed Stella's refined sense of humour which is boosted by her authoritative tone in her observations about life. The magnetism of Stella was arresting.

STELLA

Working at home or at the office did not push many life buttons for the long-serving, 52-year-old business data manager. A steady income and security had enabled her to own a home, and to raise and educate daughter Clare, who was still living at home and working in the city as a customer service officer. Stella's long-term employer, a nation-wide electrical retailer, rates her data management skills highly and has never demurred from financially accommodating her absences including maternity leave, illness and extended leave for travel and family problems. Work demands, the support of her daughter and the running of her household have been at a social cost to friendships, romance, and personal indulgences.

Work and home have marooned her from the emotional pulses of companionship and any revitalising intimacy. In her work she had built strong personal networks and through social and business meetings she sensed she was respected as a valued colleague and a smart professional. The odd innocent flirtation signalled that age had not been a barrier to attract attention from male associates.

A social outlet for Stella had been gardening which had been a release from the sterility of work and the chores of housework. Gardening had introduced her to a stimulating world where cultivation and botanical investigation provided absorbing diversions around her Homebush home.

Her flourishing garden contrasts with a neighbour's bare-concreted front garden which is occupied by four vehicles of the adult-laden family. Also off-putting is their paved backyard, covered with extensive awnings which harbour the lingering smells of weekend outdoor cooking. Attending floral shows and gardening exhibitions for the last two years has given Stella an opportunity to channel and focus her leisure time and escape Homebush's growing dreariness. Whilst they provide social opportunities no new friendship had emerged.

Stella had only rare opportunities, through her daughter's teenage and early adult years, to socialise. There were short encounters with several unattached male work colleagues but she found the experiences very shallow and unfruitful. Her disappointment, she reflected, may have been attributed to comparisons made with her three-year romance with Clare's father, a charming devil, a great lover and the ultimate romantic. But like her favourite dying camelia in her garden he had departed permanently. Later it was found that this was for an interstate romantic tryst. He left a pregnant, heart-broken, and emotionally wounded Stella, who used her pregnancy to cushion disillusionment and allowed pending motherhood arrangements to divert thoughts about the shattered romance.

A visit to an indoor flower exhibition unsettled Stella when she saw her image in a long mirror at the exhibition entrance. She saw a conservatively dressed middle-aged woman whose appearance put her in a higher maturity category. This was accentuated when she ran into an old college friend whose modern dress, coiffure and poise seemed to take years off her age. While not normally concerned about the modernity of her apparel this encounter made Stella take action to improve her wardrobe and attend to her appearance when out and about. A restyled Stella was quickly produced.

On a recommendation from a work mate Stella paid regular visits to the garden centre to build her plant repertoire and garden. At first, she did not gravitate to Bonnie's area but she found she was drawn to it by the personality of Bonnie and had made it a habit to call by, chat and buy the odd seedling. She felt a strong unaccountable attraction to Bonnie growing at every encounter. And then she surprised herself by inviting Bonnie to join her for coffee.

There were aspects of Bonnie's character that impressed and there was something alluring about her strong physicality and her slightly lisped enunciation. The openness and welcoming in Bonnie's demeanour alerted Stella's desire to interact with another adult. Getting a sense of a stranger's character is trying in most situations but surprisingly Stella found this not so in Bonnie's case. When conversing it seemed that her inner spirit easily flowed transmitting a warm and genuine depth of character. And she had a sense that Bonnie was likewise impacted by her presence. She thought that a female friendship, often highlighted in romantic fiction books and magazines, could be within her grasp.

Daughter Clare sensed something was afoot following her mother's many visits to the garden centre.

Observing Stella's attention to her attire and appearance and a surprising lift in enthusiasm in managing her daily affairs confirmed her suspicions. Conversations about the challenges of work also disappeared over the evening meals. Clare's suspicions were further confirmed when Stella announced that her forthcoming mountain visit would be with someone called Bonnie, a lady she met at the centre. Clare thought there is no accounting for what will lift one's spirits.

A point of contrast between Bonnie and Stella was in their home habits and agendas. On house management Bonnie kept a casual approach whilst Stella, despite hindrance from Clare, maintained a more fastidious regime. Both homes had no religious symbols evident. Stella had kept a fleeting link with her Anglican roots and enjoyed choir performances on the radio. Bonnie's furnishings were more cluttered and casual array and there is always a back-log of laundry. Stella followed an interior decorator's tidiness template for placement, location, and storage. Both houses were devoid of photos of former partners.

The orderliness of Stella's home sharply contrasted with Bonnie's. However, both suffered the same disorder in the kitchens and bathrooms. Both bathrooms reflected the intrusions of adult children where cabinet disarray, sink spillage remnants, shampoo storage disorder and undisposed toilet roll cylinders were encountered. Likewise, their kitchens share the bathroom experiences where timely clean ups, storage, and garbage disposal, despite frequent reminders, suffer inattention. Stella's reprimanding outweighed Bonnie's.

Colleagues comparing them might convey that Bonnie was more extrovert, excitable, casual, and unquestioning in social situations. To many she simply left an impression of goodness. Stella had a hesitant and a judgemental disposition and newcomers often found her forceful through keeping social interactions somewhat measured. Both possessed engaging personalities best revealed when in familiar surrounds and gatherings. If anything, Bonnie displayed warmth and openness where Stella could be more circumspect in her encounters. Outwardly an observer could infer that they would be unsuited as friends. And on broader sensual dimensions they also could be judged to be incompatible.

Stella has pondered that, since college days, she really had no close girlfriends and wondered whether this was true for most urban women tied to family, work, and an ever-changing neighbourhood. At work she noted that the banter about men with boyfriends had a queer sexual connotation but for women, with girlfriends, the equivalent connotation was not apparent. She was hopeful that a friendship with Bonnie might lead to a more enriching social life.

The mountain visit was not well received by Clare querying whether Stella was perhaps too keen to go away and to share accommodation with a casual acquaintance. Clare's comments were interpreted by Stella as tinged with selfishness or jealousy given Clare's limited social connections with her age group - a bit of a loner she thought. Stella was aware that single parents, with a single, long-homed, adult offspring, might encounter a possessiveness or selfishness leading to envy or resentment whenever the parent had a new opportunity for friendship. It was as if some permanent, implied companionship knot was being untied and relationships threatened.

Clare's sense of disquiet was heightened when Bonnie called by one evening to give Stella some last-gasp seedlings scheduled for disposal by the centre. Clare, possessing a withering frown, was surprised by her mother's warmth of greeting and her eagerness to invite Bonnie in for a drink. Clare's physical assessment radar did not blip positive as she scanned a Bonnie in her work outfit. Unkind adjectives ran through her mind; chalky or bleached hair, moderate paunch, fatty arms, heavy neck, thinly eye-browed, smallish torso, and bulgy breasts. She reluctantly greeted Bonnie and made her escape to her bedroom. Lively chatter from the lounge room confirmed Clare's fear that the seeds of friendship had been sown. And this was further supported when Clare looked out the window to see her mother warmly farewelling Bonnie at the front gate.

ON THEIR WAY

Both Stella and Bonnie prepared for the weekend away.

It was arranged that Stella would pick up Bonnie early Saturday morning for the drive to their mountain motel in Leura. They agreed to share a room and Stella would make the booking for a Saturday night stay. Stella had also booked dinner at a Leura bistro. They would return home on Sunday night.

Bonnie found it a challenge to decide what to pack for an overnight stay and for day wear. Her recent purchases of casual clothes seemed not right for the temperamental climate of the mountains. She added a jersey and her bright coloured anorak to cover cooler weather. As an avid wearer of shortie pyjamas, she reflected that they might not be appropriate for a shared room opting for her long blue nightie which was last worn when she and Jason went to Ballina to stay with relatives. She packed a couple of coloured bandanas to add a splash of brightness for day visits. The only jewellery taken would be her favourite bangle with its intricate pattern based on an Aboriginal motif. Apart from walking shoes she packed her low-heeled sandals for dining out.

Jason's mood was acidic on Friday and wanted to know if there were provisions for his weekend meals. A slack and indifferent shopper, Jason had always left all food shopping to his mother. Bonnie simply pointed to his adult status and to look after himself. She was forever amazed at his dependency on her, even though for the past two years she had insisted that he do his own washing, arrange his own meals, and maintain some routine of cleaning his own room.

Perhaps it had not been a good idea to limit Jason's time with his father throughout his upbringing. These are the dividends I am reaping for my lax and indulgent parenting, Bonnie thought.

Usually, Bonnie was a last-minute packer for away trips but this time she double checked her clothing and toiletries before retiring. Normally a sound sleeper Bonnie found it difficult to settle as she thought about the trip, worrying whether the venture with Stella would turn out well for advancing friendship. Joining company with other people had never been a problem for Bonnie who was at ease in all kinds of social settings. However, this trip made Bonnie uneasy.

Stella finished work early and went to her salon to restyle her hair. Her conversation in the salon, normally minimal, was very chatty, surprising her regular stylist. An approving smile and long review in the mirror indicated that Stella was pleased with the result.

A look of surprise greeted Stella when Clare returned from work. She thought her mother had overstepped the mark hair-style wise, and looked a bit too shorn. Clare made no comment and noted also that Stella had spent an inordinate amount of time in the bathroom before she retired to her bedroom. The previous night she laid out the clothes for the trip, preferring dressy skirts and blouses to slacks which she often wore to outdoor events. Stella had noted that, on a previous Spring trip to the mountains, most woman on the golf course near her accommodation played in skirts and looked healthier and stronger that their trousered partners. She set aside her Ecco casual shoes for day wear and her favourite Sandler high heels for dining out.

Stella had spent much time thinking about how it would work out with Bonnie as a travel companion. She saw no reason for it not to be a pleasant weekend and expected Bonnie to enjoy the garden visits. Settling down for her bedside reading, she paused from time to time to think how their sharing would fare and what might be the surprise aspects of Bonnie. Connecting socially with others had its hitches and obstacles but, with Bonnie, for the moment, she had no such reservation.

Saturday morning greeted Stella with sparkling fresh Spring air as she packed her car and gave her plants a quick hose. Clare, a late riser at weekends, had not appeared. They rarely acknowledged each other when leaving home nor advised any times of return. Sometimes they prepared their own evening meals. Clare at weekends often wore safari themed pyjamas till early afternoon, spending time on a sofa texting other worlds. Her frayed track suit was her other lolling about attire on weekends. All her attire reflected limited taste for colour and fit. Stella, who spent a lot of time with Clare in encouraging modern standards in style and dress, just hated her attire inattention. Stella had given up on advice on wardrobe and silently disapproved of Clare's ill-fitting florals from on-line sales.

It was around 8 am when Stella reached Bonnie's house. Bonnie opened the door before Stella knocked and collected her bag by the doorway. They commented on the fine day that greeted them and Bonnie complimented Stella on her high-collared turquoise blouse and beautiful ear rings. Stella reciprocated by adoring her richly decorated bandana. After a quick hug they sped off in Stella's Honda. Bonnie had a stupid thought they could be likened to the film characters, Thelma and Louise, dashing forth to escape their households to explore the world. Stella's classic music radio selection smartly quashed this imagery.

Sydney's western suburbs slipped by as they zoomed along the motorway heading for the mountains in the distance. As they headed westwards clumps of crowded housing estates appeared, jammed in on minute frontage and sections, and suffering metal-fenced yards, claustrophobic dwarf-like gardens and a rear garden unable to host backyard cricket. Arrogant basketball hoops on garage fronts gave an 'up-yours' to cricket. Patches of scrubby woodland, seemingly yearning for a return of long-exterminated native bushland, dotted the vista.

Bonnie could not get over the tidiness of Stella's car. The cabin was spotless and there was nothing on the backseat since Stella had stowed all their luggage in the boot. Even the floor carpet looked new and there was no dust on the dash. Bonnie made a mental note to tidy her car which Jason refuses to clean after prolonged use. Their 80 kmh felt slow as overtaking trucks prompted Stella to raise her ire about the dangers posed by these menacing, hustling road monsters.

They stopped for a break and coffee, once they'd completed the first ascent of the mountains. The café had a feel of yesterday with an old-fashioned cake display cabinet and laminated table tops with sugar, salt and pepper dispensers reigning their centres. Ordering their coffees became a challenge as the youthful tattooed server was engaged in a long conversation with her customer about the nearby national park. Their coffees proved disappointing. They half-expected so, as the coffee brand had a poor reputation and was rarely served in suburban cafes. Stella's speculation and trepidation about the wash room proved correct having encountered a cracked wash basin, a wobbly toilet seat and a mal-functioning hand-dryer.

When they returned to the highway Stella predicted they would get to their motel by noon.

Bonnie, now in a total relaxed mood, kept glancing over noting how Stella sat very upright in a chauffeur style, and occasionally broke out in an unprompted smile. From time to time one hand tapped the steering wheel and the other flicked her earring. She noted the sharpness of her features and her svelteness became more apparent when looking side on. There was a stately and underlying vigour in her physical character reflected in the way she commanded the vehicle and directed conversation. Bonnie sensed also there was a tightened emotional spring encased in Stella that was seeking release.

Stella enjoyed the freedom of the road accompanied by this agreeable travel companion to share the ascending highway even though progress was slowed by interminable traffic lights, speed zones and faltering day trippers. Especially pleasing was the warmth and natural affability Bonnie displayed and her ability to join conversation with lively and divergent observations, supplemented by discerning humour. Stella was stirred by the physical presence of Bonnie beside her and every movement of Bonnie in her seat transmitted a kind of unseen welcoming aura of belonging and sunniness. Stella was buoyed.

The intra mountain landscape along the highway no longer inspired Stella. Bushland and rocky outcrops were being obscured by commercial development, road signage, obliterating embankments, graffitied retaining walls, and unsightly shopping precincts. Multiple changes in road speed zones were frustrating. Emerging from a curve in the highway no longer gave a panoramic uplift. Stella could not wait to get to the outskirts of Leura and to settle into the motel. Bonnie, leafing through the promotional material for the exhibits, noted that there were three display gardens forming the exhibition. She hoped that they were well away from the highway which dulled the experience of the mountain environment.

The motel was in a leafy street. It had a tight set of brick units embraced by a pot-holed parking forecourt. Room 11 suffered an entrance doormat worn and tatty from many years of duty. The air-conditioned room greeted them with an air-freshened sandalwood odour which lingered in the tea-making alcove and loitered in the bathroom. The two single beds, a stride pace apart, had black woven metal bedheads overlooking strawberry-coloured bed covers whose frayed state suggested long service. The floor was newly carpeted and the walls had two framed pictures of gumtrees shrouded with snow. The bathroom had two mirrors, one above the basin cabinet and a full length one behind the door. A glassed-shower cubicle skulked in the corner marred by black mildew accumulated around its frames. Generous white towels posed in an open cabinet topped by a faded-white washbasin.

Stella gave Bonnie the choice of beds. Bonnie did a sitting-testing bounce on both and opted for the nearest to the door. They stowed their bags after removing their toiletry kits and the clothes to be hung. After a short ablution they drove to a nearby café for a snack before commencing the garden visits. Bonnie noticed that Stella had refreshed her make up and had removed her earrings. Her face had perceptively changed and seemed to be brighter with the aid of applied blush on her cheeks.

The café contained old-style milk bar cubicles recently painted to match the bluish décor of the interior. Looking around, Bonnie noted that there were mainly groups of three to four older lady patrons advancing through nutty salads, toasted sandwiches or, on advice from the waitress, something called 'three-sisters' crepes. She noted too that, common among the groups, there were overbearing types dominating the chatter. Several ladies wore Greek fisherman caps and sleeveless puffer jackets. Salads were ordered accompanied by some sparkling mineral water. Bonnie was struck by Stella's gusto in relishing her salad.

Their afternoon agenda was two gardens harbouring bulb flourishes and woody shrubs gaining their Spring foliage. Bonnie impressed Stella with her botanical knowledge and her authority about whether these plants would do well in the garden at Homebush. As they stood around the garden beds, Stella occasionally leaned into Bonnie to comment quietly on a bulb bloom or a shrub shape. This meant that their faces brushed. Bonnie was surprised that she registered a slight heart thump. She noticed that, despite the movement around the gardens, Stella's scent lingered on her face. The arresting scent enfolded her again when they gave their phones to a fellow visitor to phone-photo shoot them as they sat together in a garden gazebo.

On the drive back to the motel Stella talked non-stop about the gardens and how their beauty penetrated your senses reminding of renewal and a new season of life to experience. Bonnie agreed adding that, in her nursery job, she often marvelled at the capacity of a humble seed to bring forth blooms of brilliance and magnificence.

They both decided to shower and change before dining out. Stella showered first as Bonnie laid out her clothes for the evening. The first thing Bonnie noticed when Stella emerged from the bathroom was the trimness of Stella which was emphasised by her stylish underwear. She could not believe how well they appeared to complement her torso and legs. Stella reminded Bonnie that the shower head was clogged and a full spray was not possible. As Bonnie towelled, she looked down at her change of underwear resting on the basin cabinet and thought about their relative drabness. Before leaving she pirouetted in the front of the mirror to check how her underwear looked. She adjusted her bra to try to minimise fullness. Bonnie had comfortably shared rooms with female colleagues and now found herself unaccountably apprehensive about her figure as she crossed the room to collect her dress laid out on the bed.

While finalising their make-up Stella observed how good it was to get away from work and home and get transported into a different world. She thanked Bonnie for joining her and said it was so pleasing to share the weekend with her. Bonnie felt also that this was great experience observing how wonderful it was to break from her humdrum life and be able to enjoy adult company. As they talked both Bonnie and Stella felt a mutuality being formed tinged with a sensual magnetism which both were hesitant to express.

Both could not believe the restaurant had earned accolades from food critics. The menu was expensively ordinary and choices limited. For a spring weekend the patronage was very poor with many tables empty. Stella suggested that they have an entrée only and move onto a nearby wine bar where an outside blackboard advertised tapas-styled food. The waitress made no comment when they left after dispatching the mediocre garnished-devilled, three-prawn entrees.

The wine bar was noisy and full of happy folk. They secured stools at the back of the bar and ordered terrine and ham platters. Stella suggested a pinot-gris to go with the food. The lively wine-infused atmosphere swept them up producing a non-stop chat about their lives, former partners, and the burden of adult children. As the night progressed a relaxing Stella and relaxed Bonnie would have conveyed to those around them that they were great mates. By 10.30 they decided to return to the motel and phoned for a taxi. Their departure was interrupted by a woman who warmly greeted Stella asking about her well-being and promised to catch up for a lunch. Bonnie had a tinge of jealously when Stella mentioned that the greeter was a former work mate.

Back at the motel Bonnie, already in bed, mentioned how she enjoyed the night and the chance to relax. Stella had removed her shoes, visited the bathroom, hung up her outfit and now was stretched out on the bed in her underwear. To Bonnie, Stella appeared mildly inebriated as she rambled on about her worries about her daughter. Bonnie could not unfix her gaze on Stella 's flat midriff and plaster-pale body. Stella eventually changed into a T-nightie and bade goodnight. Images of Stella undermined Bonnie's attempt to sleep.

Stella was showered and dressed when Bonnie emerged from her dreamy sleep. A cup of tea was delivered to her bedside table. Stella commented how peaceful and serene she looked and pointed out the glorious weather they would be enjoying.

As Bonnie was towelling herself after showering Stella knocked on the bathroom door and asked if she could enter to grab items from her toilet bag. While Stella collected the bag Bonnie hung up her towel and collected her underwear. Stella could not avert her gaze from Bonnie's image in the mirror where her pinkness and innocent vanity brought on unexpected arousal. The tapering of pinkness to slight tan, from thighs to legs, was especially arresting. And what surprised her was how she admired the strength implied in this nakedness. A surprised and glowing Stella left the room to regain some balance to her feelings.

Bonnie had noted Stella's gaze and felt her own tingling response. Neither commented on their feelings as they packed to leave the motel to greet the mountain greenery.

The morning's viewing seemed to pass in a flash. After the motel both women felt they were being transported into another universe of senses. They could not believe how the physical body wonderfully complemented their positive character images. It was as if their reactions and stirrings were affirmed. And this preyed on their minds as they travelled down the mountains to experience another week of mundane encounters.

Approaching Bonnie's home, silence reigned as they navigated the dreary Ryde streets. The emotional load built up in the short weekend interlude seemed to pitch them in a dreamy state of wondering what could unfold if their friendship progressed. Stella broke the silence when they reached Bonnie's house. She asked Bonnie if she would like to experience the Canberra Floriade at the end of the month. Trying to suppress her delight Bonnie said this would be a great treat and, subject to checking her work roster, she would love to come. As she left the car Bonnie leaned over to give Stella a farewell kiss on her cheek which however lodged on Stella's lips who, in farewelling, had turned to face toward Bonnie. Both could not believe how startled they were of its gripping impact on their feelings.

ROMANCE BLOOMS

Work at the garden centre seemed to drag as Bonnie cast her thoughts to the forthcoming Canberra visit.

Conscious of her figure Bonnie took every opportunity to walk around the centre as well as modifying her diet. She collected the seedling trolleys from the loading dock and, when there were no customers around, she undertook some torso exercises in the hope of securing a slimmer profile. She closely observed how some of her more stylish middle-aged female customers' outfits were arranged, allowing the plumper ones to offset their fullness through clever colour and style coordination. And during lunch breaks she now became an avid reader of health and fashion magazines left in the staffroom. She particularly noticed new styles of lingerie resolving to invest in new sets before Canberra.

At home, Bonnie now found she spent more time reflecting about the exchanges with Stella and pondered the unknown with her feelings heading into untried sensual waters. Sensuality, in the sexual realm, had long been dormant and was flattened by her failed marriage. The electricity encountered with Stella stirred her. Were the incidences and joy of bi-sexuality and women love, now widely discussed in the media, more prevalent and appealing than she thought? And considering the relationship explorations in documentaries and films viewed on her streaming service programs, she knew that such same-sex coupling had wide and growing acceptance.

Bonnie pondered again whether Stella was likewise affected. The problem was that she had no confidant with whom she could explore her feelings. There was some comfort drawn by the public declarations by several high-profile married women who had redirected their lives and formed new partnerships They had jettisoned male partners and heterosexuality in favour of loving same-sex partnerships. She was unsure whether some of the commentary was more to do with unsatisfied relationships than with finding new ways to express love.

As she mused about her feelings for Stella, Bonnie thought about her workmate, Anne, in an open lesbian relationship, and who appeared very happy with life. At coffee breaks Anne regaled stories of her adventures and socialising which was a foreign world to Bonnie. Once she saw Anne's partner collect her from work and was amazed at their similarities in looks and appearance. They shared angular bodies but differed in their face shape and hair style. Her partner's exaggerated loping stride was noticeable and which Bonnie viewed as unladylike.

Jason, noted that his mother was unusually buoyant following the weekend away and there was a lightness in her demeanour in the weeks following. There seemed more attention to her appearance especially her hair and more fuss about her work clothes. The announcement of the Canberra trip drew no comment except for remarking how her behaviour seemed off-beat of late.

Stella thought that her reactions to Bonnie were not surprising, given the relationship drought she had experienced. She had a strong inkling that Bonnie could be the right person to embark on a journey of sharing and the signs were positive in this regard. It seemed that Bonnie invited closeness. And this was underlined by the encounters over the past weekend and the swirl of excitement experienced when her eyes swallowed the naked Bonnie.

Not normally considering her horoscope, Stella noted that her star sign had projected opportunities for high romance and an unexpected turn of events, all leading to surprises in relationships and travel. This strangely affirmed the emotional undertow pulling Stella into a sensual whirlpool.

The gamble to invite to Canberra had paid off. Stella was now imagining how the relationship would be furthered and what direction it would take. She surprised herself in her drive to befriend Bonnie. And wondered whether it would lead to deep friendship and intimate moments. This was still untested territory for Stella. She thought her usual self-confidence, displayed when intimate with former male friends, might be found wanting. Nevertheless, there was a kind of emotional urgency permeating Stella who was becoming transfixed by the possible encounters with Bonnie.

Stella felt she needed a further audit of her physical appearance to impress and beguile. A view in the mirror did not suggest any change. She had noted that her scant pubic hair seemed to compliment her trim torso, her shoulders and hips were in symmetry and maybe her face would benefit from fuller lips. Former intimate times with males had left her with an impression that she had a body designed to excite and she had an uncommon capacity of sexual resilience. Maybe some new facial cosmetic touches and striking nail paint were worth considering.

Daughter Clare, aware of the Canberra plans, became more unsettled by her mother's interest in Bonnie. What did she see in Bonnie? Clare, an incurable scoffer, could not sense any appeal in her character and physique. On the beauty scale Bonnie seemed to be average - a typical middle-aged woman, burdened with a thickness of body and with breasts and buttocks emphasising dumpiness. Clare, with a quite acidulous aside to herself, gave her mother a contemptuous look whenever she was on the phone with Bonnie. There was certainly a current of warmth and joy being emitted by her mother.

Whatever hesitancy Stella and Bonnie had about their relationship, they both felt that any negativity offered by Clare or Jason no longer mattered. While they had natural cautiousness about the direction of their friendship, opposition from their children would not be a deterrence. They were not going to derail an opportunity to live and build a rewarding intimacy. But there was an overhang of their failed relationships which generated some nervousness about their fate together.

For Bonnie the early years of marriage had delivered moments of happiness and immersion in home building and child rearing. Initially her husband had been reliable, attentive in household commitments and seemed to enjoy the partnering pathway. A yawning gap however appeared when she experienced his growing detachment from child rearing and disinterest in her welfare. There was no longer the healthy throb of love and relations fell into a sharp downward spiral. They divorced and Bonnie harboured uncertainties about her contributions to marriage failure. And she did wonder whether this experience had deterred or precluded her from seeking more close friendship opportunities.

The loss of an intense romance and its aftermath had changed Stella's approach to relationships. When they occurred, she treated them casually and with some indifference. She had become adept at withholding expressions of passion and had no compunction in terminating affairs. And she began to doubt whether males could ever supply the closeness that real sharing supplies. This coolness suspended her natural yearnings for intimacy. Meaningful partnering ambitions fell into fallow. In a sense she had become adrift disregarding opportunities for socialising where an anchorage for emotional links could emerge.

JASON AND CLARE

The moment Clare saw Jason delivering Bonnie to do some gardening with Stella she felt mildly repulsed but intrigued. She had answered the door when Jason had brought some indoor pot plants from his boot while Bonnie went into the yard to greet Stella. His greeting was the epitome of awkwardness propelled by shyness. Clare, in her track suit, asked Jason if he would like a coffee while their mothers gardened.

The balding Jason's 169cms was overshadowed by lanky Clare's 177cms.

Jason's rounded head sat on a compact torso supported by stumpy legs. Any personality he possessed was hindered by a small balloon of a face, bulbous eyes, heavy lips, and a whisper of a moustache. An occasional mournful expression together with a nasal voice, reminiscent of the crackle of post pubescence, did not help his appeal and personality. Athletics was never his forte and he told Clare that he enjoyed the copious TV streaming services pouring out his favourite Sci-Fi and American comedy shows. The only setbacks to his tidy, clean attire were hands as pudgy as batting gloves and long distorted toes protesting the confines of his walking sandals

Clare's exuded length was emphasised by her boniness. A long oval face, a string bean body, high waist, and leggy legs were apparent despite her hooded track suit shroud. The pointy nose, deep set eyes, short brown hair, and heavily lobed ears all added to the affect of leanness. But from the thin frame came a muted husky voice which became emphatic through hand gestures abetted by her long fingers. Her nails were unpainted. She related how her work was a pain while life with Stella was sometimes trying. One day she hoped to go abroad to visit Italy to sample the antiquities.

Jason had an occasional girlfriend but was still a virgin. He found it difficult to approach and befriend women whilst Clare had some short periods of dating. Despite her eagerness to find love she ended up with sexual encounters but no prospect for permanent partnering or marriage. She continued to seek answers why males did not respond to her emotional and sexual generosity and their reluctance to sustain a relationship with her. A female colleague told Clare that she scared off blokes because she was highly opinionated. She claimed that Clare had the glacier attributes of a conniving courtesan. Clare occasionally resorted to masturbation to provide sexual relief.

The conversation lingered on as their mothers worked in the garden. Despite the pauses in talking, it became apparent that, outside work, both had little social life. Bonnie thought Jason was socially repressed. Their nervousness and pride precluded any admission that they were lonely.

Clare discovered that Jason did not share his mother's gardening interest and that his work was tiresome. As the conversation meandered Clare felt that Jason was enjoying their chat. She was being drawn into his film universe and being struck by his choice of favourite programs. Jason, found himself being intrigued both by her outlook and elongated anatomy. He found Clare's facial characteristics reminded him of the angular beauty of some of the female depictions in ancient Egyptian drawings. Her hand movements were strangely beguiling. He surprised himself on how he reacted given his rare exchanges with women of his age group.

Movement outside indicated that the Canberra-bound gardeners were coming in for a coffee. On a leap of hope Jason asked Clare whether she would like to go to an outstanding Sci fi movie on Sunday week in the cinema complex of a major shopping mall. Clare was jolted by this invite and tried to think of a kind way to decline. But in a moment of weakness or desperation she said that her Sunday was free and she would like to go.

Jason drove off to return home amazed that his invite had been accepted. He tried to imagine why she accepted given that they had only just met. He then considered that this was a mistake and pondered what might ensue. Clare cursed herself for accepting but given that there was another empty Sunday in the offing felt there would be little harm in going along.

Over the week both Jason and Clare ruminated about each other. For Jason there was excitement but for Clare it was a feeling of regret. Many times, she was tempted to phone to cancel the date.

It had been a long time since Jason had been out with a woman. He found excitement in female company but had never been able to nail a lasting relationship. Fantasies about love and sex were always to the fore. Visions of Clare emerged finding it difficult to frame her anatomical landscape. Did her lankiness imply a body of subdued contours, he mused? He had seen plenty of nudity on screen and accidentally of his mother when passing her bedroom. His lack of female company meant that his semen output remained in bed or in the shower recess. The arousal impact of the proximity of real female bosoms, pubic plumages and buttocks remained in the realm of fantasy.

Clare's inclination to date was on a downward slope. She harboured some bitterness about the dating game. In previous relationships she was an eager participant in sex and found she responded so well that one or two of her partners commented on her high register whimpering. Clare felt that her long legs gave her an advantage for prolonged coupling. But even this had not secured permanent partnering. Jason was not the sort of male she would ever contemplate socialising with. His height was a drawback as was the absence of any pulse of sexiness. She rated him low on the sensory scale. Whether she would try to glamorise herself for the Sunday outing remained open.

Jason did not mention to Bonnie that he had a movie date on Sunday when asking for use of the car. Sneakers and jeans were normally set aside for his date wardrobe but were now replaced by new chinos, rarely-worn brown shoes and a button-down casual pink shirt given as a Christmas present. He had applied some yuletide after-shave which he had never used. As he finished up in the bathroom, he cursed his shortness attributed to his father's diminutive family. While he had tried elevated shoes for a time, he found them somewhat ridiculous and demeaning. He had arranged to meet Clare at a shopping mall's food court for a coffee before taking in the movie.

Clare let Stella know she was going to do some shopping and may take a movie. Stella noted that Clare wore her usual jeans and sloppy joe with an animal motif. There was no makeup and adornment resided in some several large stone rings on the fingers of both hands. Clare had resolved not to try to dress-up for this reluctant outing. Fancy underwear was not on the agenda, and she had, at the last moment, decided to wear a new bra from an unworn lingerie set. When dressing, her usual silent gripe about the unfairness of inheriting small breasts, did not arise.

The crush of the mall's Sunday shopping throng did not hinder Jason's sighting of Clare as she alighted from the escalator adjacent to the coffee shop where he was seated. It seemed to Clare that Jason was slightly nervy as he enquired about her week's happenings. She directed the conversation to the movie seeking some background on why it was outstanding. As Jason burbled on the noise of the nearby coffee and food court patrons began to annoy her. Intertwined with the loud yabbering of some seniors was the clamouring of parents curtailing the energies of their young charges as well as the penetrating twittering voices of the hordes of Sunday munchers.

They walked upstairs to the movie complex. Clare hoped they would not encounter any of her work associates as they traversed the foyer. Tickets were purchased while Clare excused herself to freshen up. She stood in the cloakroom questioning why she came, but consoled herself that the movie might be fine and might, at least, counter her reluctant mood.

Settling down in their seats Clare could not help noticing the patrons seated around her. Most were male, some bearded and others with plaited hair or body jewellery. Their age range was in the twenties to thirties. Surprising her was the variety of clothing worn. T Shirts, shorts, jeans, hoodies, Hawaiian shirts, themed polos, overalls, braces and even kaftans attired the audience. In so far as she could make out, they were the only mixed couple in the audience. Although Jason had placed his hand on her armrest, she kept her arms folded to avoid any accidental tactile intimacy. She certainly did not want to convey any suggestion of amicability.

She had declined any drink or eats to sustain her through the movie but to her surprise the movie drew her in and, by the ending credits, she had been transfixed through the gadgetry, images and vistas of imaginary planets, weird lifeforms, and odd-shaped space craft. Jason sensed that Clare was relaxed and happy.

Chatting at the bar in the foyer was not an ordeal, Clare thought. She found herself exploring movie aspects with Jason who outlined the finer points of good Sci Fi film production. Jason was secretly thrilled that he had an audience and that of a female. Over a second drink Jason was mulling over the possibility of asking Clare if she would like to a do another movie sometime and perhaps dinner afterwards.

As they walked to the entrance of the centre, Clare gave Jason her other contact details and said to let her know if other good Sci Fi movies were to be screened. Jason tried to construct whether this request conveyed more than a courtesy and whether there was some interest in him apart from being a film buff and guide. He tried to think what Clare's intentions were as she boarded her bus. And did the hard squeeze of his hand in their farewell handshake convey any significance.

Try as he might Jason, in the following week, could not erase Clare from his thoughts. He contemplated what sort of relationship could emerge and wondered whether there were romantic possibilities. He even allowed thoughts of a sexual engagement, but as a novice in such matters, he could not see how he would advance it and what he would do if it unfolded. His fantasising was emboldened when streaming an adult porn TV clip. In an adult coupling scene, the seductress was unusually thin with a beanpole figure and very small breasts.

Not totally surprised Clare received a call from Jason inviting her to a pre-release of a highly rated film to be followed by dinner.

Following work on the designated Friday they met at a city bar before catching the movie. They perched by a crowded bar teeming with office workers. This mainly female assembly of chatter-boxers and braggers were intent to ensure that their prowess and experiences at work were not drowned out in the crescendo of the competing babble enhanced by alcoholic refuels. Through the noise Jason caught most of Clare's observations about the frustrations with her job and the slack management experienced. Jason's empathy with her situation encouraged her to rage further about her hopeless colleagues and, by her third wine, she was in full flight about bureaucratic dysfunctions.

This animated Clare stirred Jason. Her cutting observations seem to be in accord with her physical sharpness. Through this monologue Clare touched Jason's arm to emphasise a point and a few times her leg brushed Jason's. It seemed she was desperate to talk to counter some conversation deprivation or drought. There was an electricity or vitality in Clare being released through this demolition of her employer.

They decided to skip the movie and move onto dinner. A tipsy Clare surprised Jason when she clasped his arm on the walk to the restaurant. She continued in a non-stop barrage about her work which did not dampen Jason's growing excitement that he was on a date.

During the main course, which were strips of lamb teetering on small mounds of mashed tuber centred on over-large white plates, Clare slowed to give Jason space to reflect on life and the future. There was little levity or much information in his chatter. Jason had noted that Clare, when returning from the restroom, had attended to her make-up and that the two top buttons on her blouse were undone. He sensed there was a growing earnestness in her as she probed his views on the scope of social life and relationships. Clare pressed her right leg repeatedly against his knee. Jason wondered whether there was some sensual signal afoot. He became unsettled adjusting his sitting position as he experienced a thickening penis.

Jason accompanied Clare to her bus stop. They had an 'about to alight' quick embrace and Clare's 'let's do it again sometime' suggestion brought Jason's evening to a close.

On the way home Jason wondered whether the signalling from Clare was genuine. Clare mulled over Jason's character in the gloom of her late-night bus. He did have some redeeming aspects and he was clearly an unattached male. In the absence of any likely male, the sybaritic Clare could find a target in Jason.

Clare found herself alone at home while Stella was interstate on an assignment for work. She longed for some male company. She rang Jason to see if he was free to join her at home for a pizza and a movie she could stream. They agreed for Thursday night as Clare was on a four-day shift. Jason's acceptance was delivered with subdued delight.

Thursday night found Clare and Jason, both excited about the evening ahead, settled in to watch the movie. Clare had selected an off-shoulder blouse, bell-bottom slacks, and low-heeled sandals to wear. She chose a bra to emphasise perkiness and wore suggestive long ear rings. Jason had selected his only tailored blue shirt and tan chinos to illuminate his body.

The movie, based on a sci-fi comic book hero, failed to excite. The pizza eaters were seated on swivel easy chairs and had a small table, holding remnant pizza and wine drinks, separating the two. The conversation about the inanity of the movie was fading and Jason' s mind raced to fill a pending chatter gap. Clare sensing a collapse of conversation got up and poured more wine and invited Jason to come into the sun room where they could observe Stella's recent attempts at Bonsai.

Settling onto the sun couch Clare patted the space beside her for Jason to occupy. Clare was desperate to answer the sexual call of nature.

She probed more about Jason's social life including his friendships. It quickly emerged that Jason did not have a large social outreach which suggested to Clare that associations with females were few and far between. Placing her wine glass on the floor Clare placed her arm around Jason's shoulder, lent over delivering to a startled Jason, a full moist kiss on his unsuspecting cheek, while the other hand slipped under his tight shirt.

Jason encountered a rush of entangled thoughts and feelings unable to decide how he should physically react. Should he remain cool and unmoved, should he respond likewise and risk exposing his amateur canoodling status, or perhaps should he excuse himself on the pretence that he has a busy Friday to face at work. These were among the scenarios racing through his mind. All was resolved when Clare pushed him down on the couch and continued a foray of kisses on his neck and mouth.

A now body-throttled Jason could hardly move as an atop Clare pressed her body firmly down on the yielding novice. Clare sat up and removed her blouse and bra revealing a bony, slightly freckled torso with conical small breasts yearning for ampleness. An excited and rapidly responding Jason, overwhelmed by the sight of flesh and skin contact, spilled his seed in the confines of his chinos. He asked Clare if she could let him up so he could visit the bathroom.

Jason returned to the arousal scene to find a topless Clare sitting back and drinking her wine. Stupidly, he later thought, was to have apologised for his bathroom exit. He did not admit that he had never experienced such intense embracing. An inebriated Clare had said she only wanted to convey to Jason her momentary feeling of warmth and happiness because her actions, signalling her emotional state, came naturally as they sat together in the sunroom enjoying a pleasant evening.

Clare thought she might engage Jason further but his hesitancy and lack of composure derailed further intimacy. His amateur status had been confirmed. Remaining topless she bade farewell to Jason at the front door inviting him to phone about a future date. Retiring to her bedroom Clare thought about how stirred she was and ruing the opportunity lost for a long overdue full sexual release. What gladdened her though was the positive sign that she could still arouse a male, albeit a dumpy greenhorn.

Clare would be shocked to know that her sensual, sybaritic style was a disposition possibly inherited from Stella.

The return journey home for Jason had him reflecting what might have happened if he had more experience with women in intimate moments. Videos and magazines do not replace field experience he thought. He resolved that he would try to manage the next opportunity and somehow let Clare know of his beginner status and exploit her experience.

LOVE JOURNEY

Bonnie surveyed the Canberra hotel room and farewelled Stella, who had to visit the city centre to finalise some matters with one of her firm's clients. She welcomed the Saturday afternoon sun streaming through the window and took in the view of adjacent parkland flushed with Spring. She marvelled at being so buoyed by this weekend away with Stella. The mountain trip had unleashed feelings not experienced before, as the image and character of Stella had unshackled some wellspring, pushing her to seek some sort of intimacy with Stella. In her mind she had explored what this might entail from simple bonding to something quite deep including an engulfing intimate experience. And she understood that any emotional sharing with Stella could no longer pass as a simple companionship.

The return of Stella woke Bonnie from a little nap in the chair beside the window. Unaccustomed to daytime naps, Bonnie was surprised how easy it was and thought it was down to being relaxed and away from normality. They booked to go to a local Thai restaurant and have an early evening before taking in the Floriade on Sunday.

There was a heady atmosphere in the room as Stella took off her shoes and jacket and stood behind the seated Bonnie. Stella commented on the beautiful park and offered some wine she had brought in from her car. Soon they were chatting about Canberra and its extensive civic and recreational amenities. Stella observed that while the civic ambience was uplifting, there was however something sterile and artificial about its character which she claimed to be attributed to the public service. She found government employees had a woeful dress sense and even those, who aspired to a smart casual get-up, looked dull and cheerless. Expanding on this critique Stella satirised the pallor of the locals emphasising the colourless, anaemic, and washed-out appearance of so many public servants-many she met were simply lack-lustre. All this had Bonnie in fits of laughter.

Further wine intake found the two in full conversation flight, recounting bungles at work and in relationships. A focus were the men who were significant in their lives. They were quickly in agreement that, in early days, their naivety and misplaced trust perhaps had them believing that notable hiccups in relationships were transitory and issues were resolvable. They had a chuckle about Stella's short affairs. Soon they were in a philosophical mood, talking about what cements relationships and what would each seek from any ongoing involvement. Bonnie thought that honesty and vitality were important while openness and commitment were Stella's maxims. The wine eventually had them venturing into sensual territory. Stella thought expressions of love could be unbounded while Bonnie had an increasingly open mind on how love could be expressed and transacted.

An unsteady Stella and a merry Bonnie, arm in arm, wended their way along the footpath, to the Thai booking while suppressing laughs as Stella again lampooned the pallor and outfits of locals passing them on the footpath. They were amazed at the large number of South Asians out and about. Stella was in fine form as she recounted stories about the divorce rate in one government agency she dealt with. The most unlikely were entering their third relation-ship and the choices of partners were harvested from the same grey cohort perched behind screens. And worse the dimmest seemed attracted to the brightest. Permissive work conditions allowed some to further their assignations during office hours.

The restaurant did not match their upbeat mood. Its décor was phony and the gabble from the pallid and chubby patrons, encircling their plastic-wood tables, emitted a roaring din. The diners, gobbling up their Saturday night curry and noodle choices, did not seem to mind the noise. After sharing a green curry, the merry ladies escaped the deafening eatery whilst navigating around the outside entrance way blocked by Asiatic Uber tribesmen. The Thai sojourn did not depress their high spirits as their ramble-like stride brought them back to the hotel.

Enclosed in the elevator Bonnie found herself snuggling into a giggling Stella as she tried to recall their room floor. The rise of the elevator matched the rise of the emotions of the ascending pair.

Dawn saw the two lying naked on a bed. Stella's was face down asleep and an awake Bonnie lying on her side with one leg draped over Stella's leg. Bonnie could not believe what happened and could not believe the intensity of their love making. She could not believe what Stella orchestrated and demonstrated. The exquisite sensations still generated a quivering as she recalled the night. Stella's lithe body seemed to mould into hers and became more agitated as Stella sought out her ampleness. Responding, Stella found her touching pushed Bonnie into multiple blood-thumping releases intensifying her own reactions.

Bonnie passed her hand softly over Stella's back and, aroused, wanted to repeat, and seek more of what was experienced. She wondered, like herself, whether she was the first female sexual encounter Stella had had. Stirring,

Stella rolled over and pulled Bonnie closer. Both uttered their delight over the night's encounter. Hands began to explore their willing bodies moving quickly to the pubic mound. The intensity of Stella's rubbing found Bonnie hurling herself again into an unbelievable state of arousal.

Lying back novice Bonnie asked Stella whether it was also her first female encounter. Stella said it was but her past experience of affairs gave her some insight. One or two male acquaintances had manually aroused her following their failure to achieve penetration - my 'Casanovian flaccidites' as Stella called them. And this experience had helped their evening of lust, thought Bonnie. They laughed when Bonnie observed that in bedding each other they proved themselves to be fast learners. And who needs men they chortled.

Their morning shower together gave them more opportunities to entwine their bodies while marvelling at how their nakedness was overwhelmingly stimulating. They found humour in comparing the size differences in their breasts and nipples. The mutual physical and emotional attraction had been sealed in Canberra.

The Floriade was somewhat of an anti-climax. Unhelpful were the crowds and constant blockage of people stopping to take photos. On the drive home passenger Bonnie slipped into a dreamy reverie as Stella chatted on, occasionally caressing Bonnie's face by taking a hand off the steering wheel. The whole episode had Bonnie mentally projecting on what lay ahead while Stella mused whether a long-term loving relationship would result.

Stella tried to concentrate on the drive but pondered about the heightened impact Bonnie produced. Never had it occurred with men. Was there something about Bonnie that revealed a latent impulse to be with and be loved by a woman. And she also pondered about what their future could be.

As they approached Ryde, they agreed to having the next weekend together and go north to an apartment Stella's friend owned at the Central Coast. The story to be given to offspring is that they wanted to meet Stella's friends who ran a native plant nursery at nearby Mount White.

Bonnie found Jason glued to the TV making no attempt to ask her how Canberra went. As she busied loading the washing machine, she told him that next weekend she was going to the central coast to look at native flora nurseries which specialised in Banksias. He made no comment.

Clare gave Stella a quizzical look when told of next weekend's plans. Sensing some change in body language, Clare pressed her on the details of the Canberra trip. Trying not to be evasive Stella said that they found the Floriade a bit of a disappointment but they had a lovely dinner out on Saturday evening. She added that Bonnie was great company and they shared a common ground on many things. Drawing no comment from Stella, Clare mentioned that she had met with Jason to take in a movie.

WEEKEND

Saturday lunchtime saw Stella and Bonnie on their Central Coast apartment's balcony sitting back and enjoying glasses of pinot gris.

And in the southern coastal town of Gerringong Jason and Clare walked up the street from the rail station to a small motel Clare had booked. Their rail trip was an eyeopener to Clare, a novice rail traveller, who found south bound passengers in the carriage, an intriguing mixture. There were islander ladies with obese offspring, clusters of Asian families, teenage phone-addicted tattooed girls, elderly couples either sleeping or completing crosswords and young parents frantically controlling their restless charges. Jason remarked that these are typical weekend passengers and most would be headed for a day out on the south coast.

Up north the relaxed newly-minted lovers contrasted with the edgy Jason and the feisty Clare down south. The lovers up north were embarking on perhaps a golden highway while their offspring down south were on a rocky path with an unclear destination. Jason was heading to unknown territory with an uncertain sexual compass.

Clare had seized the last-minute opportunity to invite Jason come to Gerringong to partner her at a work colleague's wedding and a reception held there on Saturday night. Jason, reluctant at first, quickly accepted when told he would have to share her motel room given room shortages.

An anxious Jason, for the first time, would spend overnight in a room with a woman who could be a sexual predator and perhaps remove his novice status.

While Stella's friends were giving a tour of the natives in their nursery, down at the motel Clare was changing into her outfit for the occasion. Jason, sitting in a corner lounge chair, watched, with some excitement. Clare had emerged from the bathroom in her underwear and began to dress. He had never experienced such prolonged exposure. He noted that her stiff bra swaddled her breasts and her high-sided undies seemed to suggest endless thighs. Dressed, she invited comment if the dress looked fine. An affirmative followed, even though he thought the mauve dress seemed to drape too much over her willowy body and wickedly thought that she looked like a clothed clothes-horse.

Late evening a naked Bonnie was sitting in bed while a naked Stella attended to some text messages. At the motel down south, the couple had returned from the reception with a bottle of surplus champagne the hosts had supplied.

Bonnie could not take her eyes off Stella and quickly moved to caress the back of the transmitting Stella. Messages were terminated as an aroused Stella secured a writhing Bonnie.

The merry Gerringong couple filled the motel room with laughter as they joked about how awful the reception was including the appalling food, the inept MC, and the AI-inspired bridal speeches. The unshod couple were sitting on the bed swilling the champagne from the bottle. The less inebriated Clare, sensing an opportunity, pulled her dress off, retired to the bathroom and returned naked. Her skeletal frame confirmed Jason's speculation about her physique although the prominent globes of her buttocks surprised him.

The cradled central coast couple, at rest following their spooning encounter, would have been amazed at the happenings with their offspring down south.

Clare, with some prompting, urged Jason to undress and jump into bed with her. After some clasping and manoeuvring, a spilling Jason gained entry but produced a frustrated Clare. Undeterred and having given Jason a short respite, Clare, using some classic manual tricks, had Jason clamped inside and took her rightful satisfaction. A now exhausted Jason now realised what he had missed in his early adult life. And Clare was the most perfect conductor for this awakening journey.

Sunday morning saw Bonnie and Stella talking about native flora while a now erect Jason urged a sleepy Clare to return to the fray and to score some goals. For Jason there was an urgency to enjoy a meal while it lasted. The never hesitant Clare in these matters gladly enjoined, marvelling how this tubby little man could prod so well. The uncoupled were slumbering when a knock on the door by an irritated manager reminding the exhausted gnome and the exhilarated string-bean that they were well past their check-out time.

On Monday the Ryde and Homebush households were now cast into a new atmosphere as relationship development indicated that new horizons were afoot.

XMAS

Jason and Clare had long suspected that the weekend absences of their mothers together indicated a bonding relationship and most probably intimacy may have reached a natural conclusion. The ladies had agreed never to stay together over night in their homes. They agreed to tell their dependants at Xmas of their intention of becoming a couple.

Undisclosed were the meetings of Jason and Clare, who occasionally, on the pretence of work assignments, managed an overnight motel stay where Jason's oats were sewn to make up for lost time and Clare could satisfy her urge for coupling. Neither had expressed any love imperative and enjoyed the opportunity for mutually satisfying sex sessions. The meetings were notable for the absence of parleying. It was as if they were at a gym appointment to enrich their sexual prowess. Jason, had hinted at more socialising but Clare, still uncertain of her feelings about him, said for the time being, she was only comfortable with an occasional clandestine assignation.

The families were planning to get together for Christmas lunch when Stella and Bonnie would announce their decision to live together in the new year and consolidate their housing. They planned to sell the Ryde and Homebush houses and locate closer to Sydney. Jason and Clare would have to find their own accommodation.

Bonnie had some apprehension about how to disclose their relationship to family and friends. Stella, had no such fear, encouraging Bonnie to be bold and confident about their love. There is something purely divine about mature adults finding love - it is something special to rejoice and cherish was how Stella put it.

Stella had first put the partnering overture following a Melbourne Cup function at a local club. They were in a lounge area where a few patrons were sitting around ruing their losses. Bonnie was on the brink of proposing the partnership but had delayed, while she weighed up the options of how best to broach housing arrangements and the right time to advise Jason. To celebrate the acceptance, Bonnie brought two cocktails from the bar to toast their love and their commitment as a couple. They did not care whether the patrons were shocked by their lingering sealing embrace. As agreed, they would tell their offspring at Xmas.

At the garden centre Xmas party Bonnie told close colleagues about her situation and was surprised about the great reception she received. The party had none of the hi-jinks of previous years where alcohol and flirting combined to raise the amorous levels of the plant purveyors. The next day Anne and her gay colleague presented Bonnie with a gift box of body lotions and skin cremes guaranteed by Anne to pamper and enliven.

Christmas day lunch saw the four seated at Bonnie's table toasting good health and xmas greetings. Stella then announced the partnership decision adding that she and Bonnie were deeply in love and wished to share the future together in the one household. Jason seemed unmoved while Clare produced a cynical-like smirk. As the ladies embraced Jason proposed another toast congratulating the romantic mothers. An upset and crying Clare rushed from the table and headed outside for the backyard garden.

An unsettled Bonnie was assured by Stella not to concern herself. She added that Clare sometimes gets emotional especially when events occur over which she has no control. What was going through her mind now was anybody's guess. Perhaps the realisation that she would need to adjust her lifestyle, including housing, had upset her hitherto stable world, Stella surmised. Jason was about to follow Clare out but Stella asked him to let her be while adding that the outburst was not unexpected and she would adjust over time.

Jason went over to his mother and Stella and gave them a big hug. He said he was happy for them and proposed another toast for their future together. Clare returned, gathered her bag, and left without a word. Jason excused himself and left to spend Xmas night with his father.

Late that afternoon saw Bonnie and Stella both well into their cups, sprawled naked over Bonnie's bed. Stella, sensing Bonnie's concern, had plied her with more Xmas cheer resulting in a very amorous Bonnie leading Stella into her bedroom. The whole Clare episode had heightened their need for each other. Their frenzied coupling underscored their need for love and to be loved.

Boxing day afternoon witnessed a morose Clare and an irritated Stella in a tussling conversation where perspectives, on the pending partnership, were aired. Stella sensed Clare was fearful of living apart and was jealous that someone else had found a place in Stella's heart. And it was a woman she had managed to woo. This particularly stressed Clare, who seemed unravelled by her mother's decision. No amount of assuaging by Stella could convince Clare of the importance to Stella to have a female partner to share a future life.

Jason had spoken to his mother the same afternoon, unfazed both about Bonnie's decision and his future housing situation. Bonnie had said she would make provision for Jason's needs. The way he reacted to the decision with grace and maturity was especially pleasing and surprising to Bonnie.

The new year heralded changes for the loving couple and to their households. Houses were put on the market when the couple rented a riverside apartment for six months while they searched for a place to buy. Clare and Jason remained at their homes struggling to avoid open-day house buyers meandering through their rent-free realms.

The buyers fascinated Jason. They inspected cupboards, lifted rugs, opened windows, turned on lights, stomped floorboards, peered under beds, trod the lawns, tested the taps, examined foundations, and flushed the toilets. Some buyers had an entourage of friends or families who critiqued colour schemes, the size of rooms and brickwork. One buyer asked about traffic noise and neighbours' ethnicities.

Clare's pique, over her mother's action, had not waned. She continued to not understand why her mother, who revelled in men's company, had done a volte-face. No amount of thinking and reflection brought Clare to accept a physical relationship between two mature women. She resolved that she would try somehow to destabilise the relationship and bring her mother back to her senses.

The household changes had galvanised Jason into action to find a nearby rental for when he had to vacate. Clare had told him she was not thinking yet about moving from her home. Jason found the Ryde rental scene dispiriting. It had become a high-rise shambles with an assortment of towering apartments, whose ugliness was heightened by the eyesore of washing and clutter on balconies. Not the fussiest of persons, he had difficulties accepting the acrid smells of cooking wafting down the passage ways, the graffiti on some outside walls, the inactive lifts and the junk accumulated in garages spaces. And the cost of rent was especially dispiriting. During his inspections the cackle and the cacophony of the residents, emerging from behind corridor doors, simply astonished him.

Since Xmas there had been little contact between Clare and Jason. His ardour had not faded but she had fallen into a mire of resentment, which stifled relations and collapsed communications. She appeared to be exasperated by Stella's actions. Her criticisms of her mother had Jason perplexed. In vain he tried to explain the world of gender conflation where many are pursuing other avenues to express their affections and commitments. But all this did not wash with Clare.

Bonnie enjoyed their furnished apartment overlooking a stretch of the Parramatta River. They were busy chasing houses and had made an offer on a bungalow at Drummoyne. The pair felt they were on a never-ending honeymoon. All housekeeping operations seemed a doddle. And Bonnie was quite taken by Stella's gifts of jewellery. Neither had discussed horrors of menopause which was surely waiting in the wings. Bonnie was continuingly bedazzled by Stella's soft and grasping beauty while Stella found Bonnie's tenderness and willing body overwhelming.

Workmates of Stella and Bonnie noted changes in their bearing and outlook. They had informed close colleagues of their partnership. Bonnie had paid more attention to her hairstyle and clothing while her relations with colleagues and customers had increased in cordiality. Stella had become less assertive spending more time chatting with colleagues and relaxed when dealing with office problems. Stella had put a photo of her and Bonnie on her phone.

Clare's brooding and anger continued. House sale preparation was in fallow. Housekeeping was dormant. Stella had cleared out her bedroom, selected some furniture items and taken some appliances from the kitchen. Clare rarely spoke to her mother limiting the conversation to utility bills and maintenance issues. Neglect and disarray throughout the house were apparent. She continued to fume and rant privately about her mother's decision. At work her surly demeanour drew objection from her supervisor while her work associates, knowing nothing about the events at home, had virtually shunned her. She was tempted to reach out to Jason to air her feelings but resolved it was something that she would address alone.

The crunch came when Stella announced that she had arranged for interior design professionals to come to the house to arrange the décor and furnishings to increase the appeal of the house. She reminded Clare to attend to cleaning. Feeling put out Clare said she was going interstate for a month to have a break and holiday, leaving Stella to shepherd the house hunters and to deal with cleaners and agents.

The river apartment contained a happy couple. Work and family happenings did not derail their pursuit of a harmonious partnership. They had clicked. It seemed their maturity had delivered an untroubled love collaboration. Any shortcomings were relegated to the ignore bin. What surprised them both was that their openness and frankness brought no irritation. Little compliments and random embraces became part of their social in-house repertoire. And love-making fitted naturally with mood and opportunity.

Surprising them both was how fast their homes sold coinciding with their offer on the house at Drummoyne being accepted. Within four months they would have a new abode. The siblings would have to face rental life.

ADJUSTMENTS

New habitats bring surprise and challenge.

In Drummoyne the newly joined couple busied themselves with setting up house and contending with a wintry July. In Ryde Jason was depressed by his 6th floor one-bedroom apartment which gazed over and into other apartments. In Pyrmont Clare found her towering block sufficiently private to enjoy her 15th floor pad amongst the neighbouring high-rise apartment towers casting permanent shadows over the adjacent parkland and harbour. Jason and Clare were now adrift in lofty abodes where proximity to other residents yielded a surprising level of anonymity. Most of their fellow lift voyagers avoided both eye contact and greetings which added to the incognito atmosphere .

The Drummoyne brick home, double-fronted facing North East, had appealed to Stella and Bonnie because of extensive internal renovations which delivered modern features throughout. Their small front garden had Frangipani boughs waving to passers-by and the rear garden had pergolas shrouded with wisteria and bougain-villea competing for attention. A neighbour on one side was a widower in his eighties who signalled his presence by hanging out his daily washing of bed sheets and underwear. On the other side was a family with a baby daughter whose father spent many hours wheeling her stroller around the streets accompanied by two large Afghan hounds. From afar they looked like a dog sled team. This quiet haven was occasionally interrupted by the bang of a speeding vehicle hitting a nearby speed hump.

The absence of offspring delivered harmony dividends to Stella and Bonnie. Observing their routines and actions one could see that they were like 'two peas in a pod'. Outsiders could believe they were on a perpetual honeymoon. Their laughter and bright greetings to neighbours added to their image of a devoted and loving pair. Unexpectedly Stella's organisational flair melded with Bonnie's laid-back approaches producing a house of tasteful, ordered décor but with hints of casualness to make visitors feel at home. Their boudoir included a king-sized bed, luxurious curtains, a startling venetian-imaged bedspread, paintings of famous beautiful women and subdued apricot-coloured floor rugs. It beamed a serious love-nest.

Jason's apartment was stark. Transferred furniture from home did not fill the spaces. Windows were covered with venetian blinds with damaged, faded-coloured slats. The exhaust fans in the kitchen and bathroom roared. The parquet floors were pitted and marked. Somehow there was a permanent smell of disinfectant and mould throughout the rooms. His bedroom backed onto a neighbour's bedroom where occasionally he heard the culmination of the young Indian couple's successful copulation. Depressingly there was constant building noise of movement and plumbing interrupting his binging of streamed Sci-Fi shows. And Clare had dropped all communication.

Up on the 15th floor Clare revelled in the privacy of a neat spacious two-bedroom pad furnished selectively from items from Homebush. Importantly she had secured from Stella a cash gift which underwrote her rental for two years. Most of her neighbours on her floor seemed to be mixed-aged professionals whom she rarely encountered. She was alone.

An important change for Clare was to spend more money on outfits, spurred on to match the rig-outs of other female tower dwellers.

Somehow her bitterness about Stella's decision had propelled Clare to withdraw further leaving work as her only social experience. She did not contact Jason even though, on some weekends, there was a temptation to ring him. Her situation had dulled her libido as well as casting her into a continuing state of embitterment and sourness.

Jason had visited Drummoyne twice but Clare pointedly turned down invitations and kept contact with Stella through irregular and perfunctory phone calls. As she would have guessed, her behaviour was regularly discussed at Drummoyne, but Stella felt that Clare had to stew in her own resentment juices and accept that life moves on and so should hers. Bonnie had made a few suggestions for closure, but a disheartened Stella felt it was up to Clare to initiate rapprochement.

Unknown to Clare, Jason had met Imelda who was also renting in the same apartment block. He guessed she was of Filipino extraction. They had struck up a conversation as they left the apartment block to catch a bus to work. She had a hospitality job at a city hotel. Subsequent contact had Jason ratcheting up his appearance and reading up on Filipino culture after she revealed her background.

Originally, she had come to Australia to do a Nursing degree at Sydney University but left her uninspiring course because the teaching was abysmal. She switched to TAFE to complete a hospitality course which led her to her current job. Jason felt comfortable with her charm and grace. He was struck by her delicate features, petite figure, the kaleidoscope of colours in her dress, her slightly twangy accent and the perpetual wet gleam of her eye balls. Her only

Australian-based family was a married sister in Queensland and there was a relative in New Zealand.

The advent of Imelda submerged the memory of Clare. Jason joined Imelda regularly on the morning bus journey to work. And he was now her lunch companion when her shifts permitted. They frequented a park at Circular Quay enjoying the parade of the lunch time mob. He was quickly swept away into her loveliness through her engaging chatter, charm, and striking daintiness. While Jason talked about his life, Imelda kept her social and family history close to her chest. The inevitable emerged. Soon they were dating and sharing an occasional evening meal.

Their skirmishes of embracing and kissing were fleeting. The now experienced Jason respectfully held back on tactile intensity. He was unsure of the potency of her religious values. Imelda was not a provoker and there was timidity in her engagement. He could not read how she interpreted his apprehension and whether there was deep feeling towards him.

What struck Jason was how easy it was to relate to her. Weirdly he found that he changed his interpersonal routines which she had quietly prompted or introduced. He had beefed up his appearance and personal hygiene to comply with her gentle hints. She initiated embraces but her gestures seemed to limit any close intimacy clearly signalling that serious body exploration was not on her agenda.

Imelda was silent on her previous relationships but Jason mentioned that he'd had a girlfriend or two, unnamed, but not serious. Repeatedly she talked about the importance of family to her which prompted Jason to invite her to meet his mother for coffee at the garden centre one Saturday.

Jason felt the coffee meeting over a light lunch went well. Imelda knew of Bonnie's relationship with Stella.

Conversation ranged over Jason's childhood experiences, work matters and Imelda's family network. Bonnie could see that Jason was smitten. She also sensed there was an intensity in Imelda's charm including her incessant praise of the virtues of Jason who found it all a bit embarrassing. Before Bonnie left to return to work, she invited them to visit for a Sunday lunch with Stella.

Following the coffee session Jason sensed a change in Imelda. Her embracing was more intense and prolonged, her fussing became more complimentary and visits extended. The romancing and pampering went up another notch and the submissive Jason soon found himself engaged to marry. On this news a surprised Bonnie suggested that the Sunday lunch could double up as an engagement celebration. Jason had assumed Clare would not be there as part of her continued stand-off with Stella.

Imelda prepared a dinner to celebrate their commitment. Jason was overwhelmed by her greeting when entering her apartment which always surprised with its Filipino wall hangings and colourful pillows. She was knock down gorgeous. Her stylish blouse and skirt, her high heels and swirling hair arrangement had Jason reeling in amazement. After dinner Imelda was especially attentive as they sat together with a celebratory drink. A welcoming clinch soon had Jason hand slipping under her blouse and bra drawing little resistance. His descending hand, having found a surprising reactive nipple, was halted at skirt top with a reminder that this would have to wait until they were married. At no time did Imelda's hand investigate Jason's nether region.

Imelda requested that Jason meet her most important family members - her sister living in Queensland as well as her relative in Auckland. Imelda said she was permanently estranged from her parents back in Manilla and refused to elaborate the cause of this family disconnect.

Stella had called Clare to join them for lunch to celebrate Jason's engagement. A stunned Clare could not believe the news regarding Jason. She had sidelined Jason for some time. She was still buffeted by her disapproval about the twosome in Drummoyne. Now she felt doubly hurt since she thought the insipid Jason, previously captured in her sensual web, could not be retrieved at her sensual bidding. Her realm no longer included Stella or Jason.

As Bonnie sorted out the seedling trays, she reflected on how rapidly life had changed. Love had entered her and Jason's domain. It seemed like yesterday that they were the classic single mother and adult son, with no prospect of life with others. The change was momentous for both. Bonnie had to pinch herself to realise the great fortune to have a loving partner. Jason could not believe that an aimless bachelor quickly transformed from sexual novice to fiancé.

The experience of intense love surprised Stella. All the senses seem to be elevated. Inexplicably she found herself resenting how work obligations interrupted opportunities to share more time with Bonnie. Her supervisor sensed her disappointment, when required to work interstate. Phone calls and texts are no substitute for being together. The silence and attitude of Clare was certainly unnerving but, for most part, she had managed to accept Clare's communication exile. Bonnie was elated with the situation of Jason. He told her that he and Imelda were flying to Queensland to get the blessing of Imelda's sister.

The September flight to Queensland was paid by Imelda. Jason sensed that Imelda especially wanted to get her sister's approval of the choice of her knight from Ryde. A gushing overweight, bespectacled squat lady embraced Jason as he left the airbridge in Brisbane. Certainly not the spitting image of Imelda. The sister's drawling accent had been honed by 15 years of living in Queensland. Her yellow tracksuit and her coloured flip flops embellished with plastic flowers, all seemed to reflect the casualness of the north. Her hubby, a ginger-haired unshaven giant in a T shirt, footy shorts, and work boots, nearly broke Jason's fingers in a crushing handshake. Jason noted that their tanned complexion gave their skin a tough leathery look.

Carmel and Terry overwhelmed Jason with a volley of talk. There was ceaseless chatter in the cluttered Hyundai as they headed for their seaside house in Redcliffe. Imelda remained quiet as Carmel regaled Jason of the positives of the wondrous Imelda. And he found the two poodles sharing their back seat off-putting with their nauseating doggy smells and embarrassing crutch sniffing.

The early Brisbane Spring seemed roasting to Jason as he eased back in a faded blue plastic Adirondack chair on the enclosed veranda. His stubby holder, with a horse motif, attempted to keep his beer cold as he weaved through a barrage of questions from Carmel about his family and work. A silent Terry caressed the poodles whilst Imelda played with a ginger cat that had pounced from a window ledge. Potted ferns covered the peeling paint of the front wall but failed to cover mould covering the ceiling.

Jason found the fish and rice dinner stodgy noting that Imelda seemed unusually quiet through the meal. Excusing themselves Jason and Imelda took an after dinner walk along a nearby esplanade. He learnt that Carmel was divorced and had been living with Terry for six years but remained unmarried. Carmel now 45, had a son working in the mines at Emerald. Carmel kept apart from the local Filipino community because it was too close to the local church where Carmel had housekept until she resigned to avoid a crazed Polish priest.

The next morning Jason was taken aback when Imelda entered his bedroom with a cup of coffee. Her nightie and wrap hung loose and when she bent over to kiss him good morning his eyes were able to scan down her front to see her navel and the faintest of gauzy hair covering her privacy. Whether this was intentional Jason did not know because she quickly straightened and excused herself to take a shower. An excited Jason had to settle for an alerted member.

During the flight back to Sydney Imelda snuggled up to Jason letting him know that Carmel was impressed by him and observed also that his heart was in the right place. Imelda, thinking aloud, asked Jason when would he like to marry in the new year. Jason was startled. When the plane landed, he said he needed time to review the financial situation before setting definite dates. A previous nuzzling Imelda, responding in a muted steely voice, said that she would like to settle down soon and then, in the cutest way, hinted that Bonnie might be able to support them.

An increasingly pushy and excited Imelda was unsettling Jason, and marriage had some challenging issues to resolve. He was unsure whether he was cut out to be a life partner and was concerned of how compatible they would be. Imelda's attitude towards the intimate aspects of life together remained unclear. He had broached the matter of premarital sex but found Imelda confusingly evasive when he raised it with her.

A NEW YEAR

Clare did not join her mother for Xmas and New Year, and instead took a short trip to Tasmania. The gulf had persisted. Stella had talked to her about the great times with Bonnie, the wonderful Imelda, who added much to festive celebrations, and a transformed Jason, who had turned many corners including weight loss, and had become a livelier personality and conversationalist. The gift sent by Stella remained unopened. Clare's response to a Xmas phone greeting was cool and terse. Resentment burned deep in a bitter Clare.

Clare resolved to get back in the dating scene as the depressing isolation of apartment life continued through summer. There were no romantic prospects at work and amongst her fellow male tower dwellers. The males seen in the lobby or lifts were so unappealing. They all seemed to be over-earnest, characterless types. Most wore shouldered back-packs, holding goodness knows what, and suggesting they were going on some hike. She flicked through on-line dating sites but the conditions and ambit of the sites gave her little confidence and, in some respects, fear. She never joined workmates who gathered for after-work drinks on a Friday.

Her big decision, following an ad on TV, was to enrol in a part-time graduate program in Management at a nearby university in Broadway, central Sydney.

Her first subject was an early evening class on 'Business Strategy'. Around 25 students were enrolled, with a sprinkle of male and females, aged early twenties to forties, including a cohort of Indonesian students on some sponsored study program. Her South Asian lecturer was limited by his speech impediment, business knowledge, deportment, and charisma. The course used on-line case studies which were inexplicably drawn from British companies from late last century. Not one current Australian case was presented.

As the term progressed the class atmosphere degenerated and attendance became erratic. Clare was assigned to a case group with three males, an Australian, Jack, and two Indonesians. It became apparent that the Indonesians, while graduates, struggled in oral and written English. They were useless in preparing case reports. Clare and Jack, the now key writers of the reports, were soon drowning their frustration about the subject and fellow students with regular after-class drinks in the gloom of a nearby George Street pub. They complained, to no avail, to the Business Dean that the lecturer, a middle-aged male, with a UK Ph.D. degree in organisational ecology, had no business experience and was exasperating them through his substandard teaching.

What struck Clare was the whole barrenness of the university teaching precinct. Public spaces were ghost-like hallways and lobby areas occasionally occupied by an attendant or a student sitting on the floor engaged with a phone. The cheerlessness of the place mirrored the dull and unenthusiastic lecturer who seemed to resent teaching, well amplified by his irritability when students sought explanations and clarifications. Unhelpful was the haze of his fractured and murdered English. Clare could not believe how he had secured a position at the university.

A buddying process was well in train. Jack was a 39-year-old divorcee working in administration for a national import company. This 180-centimetre flat-footer comprised an overweight torso, thick black hair, a strong angular face, slightly gravelly voice, and mild stoop. He was living in a flat at Ashfield following his divorce six years ago. His wife and children were living in Victoria. Clare while hesitant at first, saw Jack as a companionship target. The approach to Jack required all the seductive guile Clare possessed.

An opportunity for getting close to Jack occurred at the end of term, when they went out to their pub to celebrate their final assessments. They did not care that their fellow case members received the same passing grade as them. As they drank into the night, they jokingly thought it was their contribution to Australia's international aid. The whole class was a farce anyway and hopefully next term would be better. A tipsy and happy Jack soon had his arm around Clare, seeking details of her private life.

A cautious Clare eased away from Jack's body trying not to indicate reserve, but not overmuch, for here could be a night of delight in the offing.

Around midnight Clare and Jack stumbled into her apartment. Still clothed Jack stood behind her on the balcony gazing below at the harbour, seemingly crushed by the glowering towers shrinking its foreshore. Jack had a hand firmly against her chest whilst nibbling at her ear. Clare backed in hard against Jack's front but felt no prod of excitement. As he pressed, she pressed but still no response from Jack. She turned, faced Jack, and then led him back into the room.

A frustrated Clare could not believe her ears when Jack said he felt a bit ill and steadied her. He excused himself as he put on his jacket whilst apologising and promising to ring to set up a dinner date the following week. He left the luckless lover's lair offering the only reward, a swiping kiss on her forehead. Clare sat on the lounge overcome with an emotion of rejection and feeling like a discarded lover.

But it seemed not at all lost when, the next day, a floral bouquet was delivered to her office with a note simply signed J. Following a call from Jack, Clare agreed to meet up in Chinatown for a meal. He was at pains to explain personally his abrupt departure.

The kitchen smell of the Lotus Moon blended well with its tatty atmosphere and its long-overdue paint job. Clare had not enjoyed her pork rolls and settled for an indifferent pinot, whilst Jack mowed through his final dish. He explained he was nervous about their encounter since it was his first date with a woman for a long time. And he did not want to give her the wrong impression by taking advantage following their imbibing. Clare reached over and grabbed Jack's hand assuring him she was relaxed finding the situation the other night agreeable. A perked-up Jack suggested that they retire to a harbour bar for a night cap.

They entered her apartment with Clare restraining herself but silently wishing for an entanglement with Jack. In the bathroom she slipped off her bra from under her blouse, checked her hair and rinsed her mouth. Standing at the kitchen bench Jack motioned to Clare to join him as she left the bathroom. He explained that he was going home but wanted to let her know that their relationship was fine but his emotional settings were not ready yet for an intimate relationship. With time he could be in a better position to commit. Clare did her best to keep calm and said that she understood but wept uncontrollably when he left.

A surprise phone call from Jack delivered Clare from a week of doldrums. He invited her to the Gold Coast at the end of month where his firm was conducting a training retreat. They could spend his last weekend there. A not too reluctant Clare said that would be a nice break for her. She pondered whether she was part of some weird romantic game Jack was playing.

Her Gold Coast flight was inhabited by a motley bunch of fun-bound 'teenadults' whose yabbering unsettled the few middle-aged couples seeking a weekend of respite from their Sydney home obligations. While waiting for her bag at the Coolangatta terminal Clare kept thinking that the weekend was a big mistake. The crush around the baggage carousel did not brighten her mood. The mass of luggage grabbers surged to collect, bumping and heaving, rarely excusing themselves as they pushed past other hovering bag gatherers. Her retrieval was impeded by a rhino-sized woman who dragged her bag through the crush whilst clutching a phone to her ear bombarding the listener with a rant about some Kevin's neglect of paying rent.

Jack, had booked a hire car to collect her and take her to his hotel at Broadbeach while his retreat finished its final day. A key was arranged for her to collect.

The room opened out on a large balcony overlooking the beach. She noted there was a king-sized bed dominating the room. A vase of roses was on a table in the snug lounge corner. Clare, was hesitant to freshen up and change before Jack returned in the evening. There was much agonising how she would greet him - whether to take a cool or warm approach on his return. But her emotional need to be desired, dispatched the need to squabble with Jack. She showered and dressed in her most fetching top and slacks. She wondered if her thong underwear was appropriate for this uncertain encounter.

Jack returned clutching two bottles of Champagne. His welcome kiss held promise. Sitting on the balcony Jack recounted the pitiable business retreat where a so-called consultant wove through materials to train staff about the positives and negatives of emotional intelligence in effective office management. Staff had advised their group manager that the training was a waste of every one's time. By the third glass, Jack was in full voice about his life while apologising for his behaviour. Encouraged by the second bottle, compliments flowed about Clare as well as more apologies for his encounters in her apartment.

The bedside clock showed 10 pm as a naked Clare and Jack took passion to its inevitable conclusion. Jack's heavy body did not impede Clare's taut thinness producing an intensity of thrust which led Jack struggling to maintain a dominance. Her propulsion knew no bounds and his throaty grunts did not put her off her game. He could not believe the power her wiry legs delivered in her slithering climaxes. At rest, Jack felt that his appendage had been through a pencil sharpener. And he was surprised how a cadaverous-like body delivered so much.

As he dozed on and off in a warm post coital glow, he recalled how his wife of ample dimensions never fully tested him. Their love making always seemed half finished and joyless. He had come to believe that marriage could be an unliveable institution, unable to deliver tolerable intimacy.

Fully wakened, he looked over at a slinky, sleepy Clare who had placed a slender hand atop his flagging member. Clare thought she had taken Jack to a place he probably had never been. And Jack seemed to confirm this, when he returned from the bathroom with a glowing smile supported by a rising phallus. By dawn, twice their bodies had not been denied.

During the night they had talked, amongst other things, about how lust underpinned both a sense of wellbeing and of being human. They thought that any decline in libidinousness was often the casualty of partners not valuing its positive contribution to feelings of self-worth.

After breakfast they took a long walk on the beach where multitudes of older people were striding along in a quest to defer elder health challenges, including cardiac trauma, paunch expansion, osteoporosis and muscle shrinkage. Women outnumbered men. Clare could not help observing that her sylph-like frame contrasted sharply with the larger ladies ploughing dumpily through the sand.

The weekend went by too fast for Clare. Jack was returning on another plane and, before farewelling, he gave her a pair of sea-motif long earrings which she wore for the journey back. Clare entered her apartment overtaken by a deep euphoria but wondering if a real Jack was encountered. Any concern she had was quickly dismissed when, before retiring, she had a call from Jack who said, in a roundabout way, that he was very drawn to her and intimated he wanted a more permanent relationship.

The following weeks saw them both dining together, attending university, enjoying her apartment, and planning weekends away. Clare had not told Stella about Jack. At university they tolerated their 'People in Society' class led by a senior female academic who tried in vain to explain esoteric theories of sociological dynamics. Fashion was not on her agenda as she wore the weirdest of long dresses full-stopped by scuffed, ankle-length brown boots. Her political orientation seemed to guide her selection of readings and commentary about social change. Her cryptic language eluded and confused most, managing, by week four, to reduce class attendance. In class Jack amused himself by keeping a tally of the number of times she repeated the words, trope and existential and how her delivery stumbled along through the frequent 'ums', 'ers, and 'ahs'.

Clare's disclosure about Jack was forced when an invitation to Jason's wedding arrived including a special plea note from Jason wanting her to attend and to bring a partner. To her surprise Jack welcomed the opportunity to meet Bonnie, Stella, and Jason all of whom had received a somewhat jaundiced appraisal from Clare. A reluctant Clare accepted, after having grudgingly repaired the rift with Stella over a Saturday morning coffee. A following cordial lunch with Bonnie and Jason also smoothed relations. The relationship with Jack and Clare's upbeat outlook and softer disposition were welcome surprises.

WEDDING

The late spring wedding was held in one of the recreation park reserves along the Parramatta River. An area was selected which was away from the dog walker traffic which, on weekends, had become of plague proportions. A strong breeze unsettled Imelda's bridal outfit. The marriage celebrant, a small lady with a pulpit-like intonation, addressed the small gathering, including Imelda's Queensland sister and brother-in-law. A New Zealand cousin of Imelda's, Isabella, added to the wedding party's numbers. A nearby picnicking group of Indian families, playing park cricket, brought a pause to proceedings when their errant cricket ball knocked over the celebrant's lectern. A calm Bonnie collected the ball and charmingly returned it to an embarrassed senior picnicker. Onlookers would note a beaming Imelda and a nervy Jason exchange vows followed by a tentative embrace to conclude proceedings.

The marriage party returned to Drummoyne for a wedding breakfast prepared by Stella and Bonnie. But the wedding couple seemed to take a back seat while a fetching Isabella circulated offering drinks and food. The 39-year-old Filipino spinster, a classic Manilla beauty, and boutique owner in Auckland, could not be denied attention. Her graceful waitress-like meanderings, unaffected by her sky-scraper high heels and a figure-hugging outfit, together with her beguiling chat, had all under her spell except for a suspicious Clare and a restless Imelda.

Following some short speeches and more congratulatory drinks Imelda and Jason 'ubered' off to a city hotel from where they would leave the next day for a honeymoon on Hayman Island, all paid for by Bonnie.

After farewelling the Queensland guests and Jack and Clare, Isabella remained applying more charm as she gave more background on Imelda's childhood and life in Australia. Apparently, Imelda had many problems with her Filipino family as well as volatile relations with a longstanding Australian boyfriend whose abusiveness led to their breakup. Imelda considered herself lucky to have met Jason who provided vital emotional support at a critical juncture in her life. Stella insisted she cancel her hotel booking, stay with them overnight and have lunch before her return to New Zealand in the afternoon.

Sobbing from the guest bedroom woke Stella at 2 am. At the door Stella asked if all was well. Isabella came to the door crying and said she was feeling gloomy. She was happy for Imelda but the occasion put into relief her own unhappiness arising from a recent failed romance. Sitting together in the lounge, Isabella revealed she had recently broken up from her lover of six years, a headmistress of a primary school. Stella comforted Isabella until she wanted to return to her room. As she bid her goodnight, Isabella hugged Stella tightly whispering how understanding Stella was and being so lucky to have Bonnie as a partner.

When Isabella arrived for breakfast Stella was quite surprised how composed and refreshed, she looked. Bonnie, told of the events of the night, was also struck by her composure. Stella offered to drive Isabella to the airport while Bonnie delivered wedding gifts to Jason's flat. As they stood at the entrance to Immigration and Customs, she embraced Stella tightly, inviting her to stay with her if she came to Auckland hoping their paths would cross again soon.

On her drive back from the airport Stella felt somewhat exhilarated by the encounter. She wondered whether Isabella was intimating more in her embraces and comments.

The honeymooners woke to a bright day for their journey north. The only concession provided by the hotel in its honeymoon suite were bottles of imported mountain-sourced water and a box of handcrafted chocolates from the Adelaide hills. The night had delivered a naked Imelda to Jason or rather Jason to Imelda. The delicateness of Imelda did not hinder her enthusiasm to join with Jason leaving him the impression that Imelda was experienced. He was not the first. Her agility and forcefulness had Jason feeling that he was the novice. The quickness of Imelda to attain her peak had him dumbfounded. Imelda said she would never disclose her past intimacies and the asked Jason to do the same.

Jason woke to find Imelda dressed and the cases ready for the airport. She urged him to shower and dress quickly so they could have breakfast before their taxi arrived. Jason noted that there was a bossy overtone not only in this request but in her last night's directional approach to lovemaking. It was all a revelation about this hitherto unknown side of her character.

Bonnie returned home to find Stella scanning the wedding photos. They talked about Isabella and Clare's link with Jack. Bonnie noted that Stella paused whenever Isabella featured in a photo while adding a comment about her vivacity. Clare was extremely fortunate to have Jack as a friend, observed Bonnie. Stella thought that Clare's relationship would not last once Jack experienced her stubbornness and authoritarian regime.

Jack spent the night with Clare where her insatiability tested his 39-year-old body. He wondered how her wiriness could deliver such repeated intensity and energy. Before returning home, Jack invited Clare to dinner the following weekend with some friends from work.

Hayman Island weather was wet and blustery. Imelda directed day-time activities with a somewhat resigned Jason tagging along. He yielded to Imelda's fancied island activities welcoming an opportunity, albeit under her baton, when he could possess her. By week two Jason felt that romance was becoming transactional and he was operating under her terms of contract. Only once did she allow him to shower with her. And she tested his patience for the inordinate time she took to dress for evening dining, while at the same time directing his choice of clothes as well as his choices on the menu. The high room rate of the resort amazed Jason who thought its dreary and tired décor was nothing like the ambience displayed on their website

At the end of a fortnight the newlyweds were back in Ryde undertaking a revamp of Jason's apartment. When Bonnie arrived, she noted that Imelda had Jason working hard on cleaning the bathroom and kitchen and rearranging furniture. Imelda quickly dispensed coffee and chat then virtually ushered Bonnie out to the carpark. Bonnie drove off sensing that Jason was now under the command of a not so admirable admiral. She knew who would be swabbing the floors in future.

SETTLING DOWN

Within a year a pattern of life emerged. In Drummoyne, Stella and Bonnie's alliance ran smoothly through a maturing romance. In Ryde, Imelda's management kept Jason up to the mark with little dissension. In Pyrmont, Clare enjoyed the regular company of Jack, who revelled in the unfailing sexual fusion. They all had companionship. Relationship scrimmages were momentary and never serious.

The announcement of Imelda' pregnancy was welcomed by all. There was a notable silence from Clare. While thrilled, Jason thought about all the challenges and ramifications for their household which had a depressing effect. Bonnie was delighted, promising to assist and provide financial support if required. Imelda took it in her stride and seemed to be unconcerned about what would unfold in the future. She would continue to work where possible, and expected Jason to increase his support of home life.

Stella saw that Bonnie was concerned about how life in Ryde would unfold. Her concern was about Jason's capacity to manage a demanding Imelda who was also putting a lot of pressure on Jason to look for better housing. A morose Jason had phoned Bonnie saying he was finding Imelda's demands and unreasonableness becoming difficult to handle. Stella could only suggest to Bonnie that Jason must take a stand when matters become too much.

Imelda's coolness towards Bonnie grew. Bonnie felt unwelcomed at Ryde, relying on Jason for news about the pregnancy. But changes were afoot with Stella. More and more Bonnie found Stella trying to lead activities, making arbitrary decisions on household operations, and forgetting to confer. She had an uncomfortable feeling that her views were being sidelined, but nevertheless was prepared to roll with life since Stella's ardour retained its intensity. On occasions Stella's bluntness and cutting observations generated concern. She had a glimpse of why Clare and Stella's relationship had had its challenges.

Bonnie's fortunes took a turn for the worst following a car accident when returning from work. Head injuries and a broken shoulder found her in Ryde hospital, where surgery and treatment had her hospitalised for a month.

Stella was a constant visitor. Jason, mostly without Imelda, came regularly. Bonnie sensed a growing despondency in Jason as he recounted his relationship with Imelda. Apart from urging him to take a firmer line with Imelda, she encouraged him to generate some private time for himself.

Jason could not believe the post-covid conditions in the hospital's operations. The number of medical staff clustered around the ward's nurse station surprised him. They seemed to be constantly huddled around their screens processing data. Out in the wards, it appeared that patient engagement was largely left to aides, cleaners, ward attendants, food servers and visitors.

A recovery setback had Bonnie in hospital for another fortnight. This depressed the usually positive Bonnie, who found the hospital conditions testing. Especially trying was the unevenness of professional care. Several nurses were at sea with procedures and one of the treating doctors was aloof, which was accentuated by his indecipherable English. In her ward she had to deal with the moaning of a lady who complained incessantly. Forever, it seemed, she was surrounded by visiting relatives ministering to her demands and being alarmed by her complaints. An attendant told Bonnie that the woman was referred to by staff as the grumpy 'duchess'.

A surprise hospital visitor was Isabella who had come to Sydney for business and to catch up with Imelda. At the insistence of Stella, she was staying at Drummoyne. They talked about the expecting couple. Isabella said that Imelda seemed at ease with her pregnancy and was lucky to have a caring husband. Bonnie was reminded again of how photogenic Isabella was as she chatted away while drawing side looks from two older males who were enjoying the distraction from the bleating 'duchess' they were visiting. Isabella mentioned she was taking Stella for dinner as a thank you for the accommodation.

The Marina harbour restaurant was quiet for a Friday night. Patrons would have noticed two animated, vivacious ladies at a corner table having a hilarious time. Both from a distance looked like fashion models, one in her fifties and the other less so. An eavesdropper would have heard their discussion about how passion had changed their lives. Observers would have noticed the younger one relishing her wine while the other was looking intensely at her dinner companion. They left the restaurant arm in arm.

Much laughter and palavering rebounded in the Drummoyne lounge room as the happy diners recalled some of their former romantic trysts. Stella even thought that some time back Jason and Clare may have had a romantic connection. Through the haze of alcohol Stella warmed to the company of the ever-entrancing Isabella who had thrown off her shoes and was reclining on a small lounge. As Stella topped up her wine glass Isabella motioned her to sit beside her. Stella surprised herself as she found herself in Isabella's embrace tumbling towards a journey of intense lust. The energetic softness of Isabella's hands had Stella yielding and reciprocating. Later, a silence from the bedroom signalled that the two had entwined to a blissful finality.

In the morning light Stella surveyed the intriguing naked Filipino dozing beside her. Plastic surgery had endowed her well. Stella felt a wave of guilt sweep over her as she thought of Bonnie. At breakfast a breezy Isabella thanked Stella for a wonderful evening making continuous references to their encounter. Stella though was a bit torn. She had a feeling that having two lovers could be rationalised, an enlightened sort of sharing, she thought. But she knew others, especially Bonnie, would not judge it that way. In a leap of daring Stella said that she would love to stay in touch with Isabella. A lingering embrace from Isabella gave the answer.

Bonnie's return from hospital and the departure of Isabella had Stella in a disclosure quandary. And the possible return of Isabella for Imelda's birth would complicate matters. She wanted to be honest with Bonnie now she had blown the trust they had created. Her thoughts diced with the secret nature of the affair and the moral issues it raised. For the moment she kept her secret.

Pressure did not relent for Bonnie. Jason's struggles with Imelda, who was to give birth shortly, and a sense that Stella generated less warmth in their interactions gave her concern. Her shoulder operation led to change in roles at the garden centre where she was assigned to a full-time clerical job in administration. And this inactivity had led to a several kilo weight gain especially around her mid-riff.

The premature arrival of the baby girl, Carmelita, diverted the households. Jason welcomed the diversion to organise the baby's nursery and to support the new mother who, surprisingly, took to the chores of handling her baby like a veteran child carer. Nothing challenged her. Imelda had the whole baby caring routine under complete control and, under her direction, Jason became the perfect nursemaid. After Imelda's feeding session Jason swung into action following Imelda's baby-rearing schedule. Stella, when visiting with Bonnie, felt that Jason did all but suckle the baby. And a saddened Bonnie agreed as Jason danced to a relentless governess-like tune.

But the cloud of stress for Bonnie did not blow away. The returning Isabella, who showered gifts on the baby, was bringing tension to her household. An attentive Stella went to extremes to host the glitzy Kiwi. Returning from work Bonnie noted that the two were always in lively conversation where a not-so-subtle flattery and subdued coquettishness were noticed. In bed at night, it seemed that her troubled shoulder gave Stella an excuse to retreat in closeness. And her goodnight embrace lacked its usual fervour.

Stella had taken leave from work to attend to some medical issues but spent some time ferrying the Kiwi to Ryde for baby watching and to boutique warehouses. They took the opportunity to have lunch together and managed an afternoon together in a motel in Glebe, where Stella could not believe the intensity and the playfulness of her Aucklander. Bonnie, increasingly uneasy by the growing relationship, remained reluctant to raise with Stella her consolidating infatuation with the Kiwi, which was being clearly telegraphed.

Before Isabella returned home, a small afternoon tea was held at Ryde to celebrate Carmelita's arrival. The reign of Imelda was in evidence as Jason scurried around organising refreshments while she sat chatting to guests. Carmelita was asleep in the nursery after having being parcelled around the guests. It was announced that there would be no christening which did not surprise given the Imelda and Jason's known agnosticism. And Imelda announced that she was returning to half time work once Jason had arranged paternal leave with his employer.

Bonnie felt she was tumbling into a web of anxiety as she pondered the destiny of Jason, the reign of Imelda, and the cooling of Stella. Particularly wounding was that Clare was absent from the whole baby merry go round. No visits to home or hospital, no congratulations, no gifts, no phone calls, no comment. A hurt Bonnie asked Stella asked about Clare's behaviour. No explanation came forth apart from 'Clare is Clare' and she is totally self-centred and engrossed with her affair with Jack. More worryingly she had to let Jason know that, because of her work commitments, there would be little opportunity to baby-sit Carmelita which seemed to catapult Jason into another level of stress.

Stella, sensing Bonnie's mood descent, announced she had booked them an island resort holiday for a week to give them a break and a diversion.

HOLIDAY

Aloft Stella and Bonnie, jammed in economy class, were each thinking about home matters - Bonnie the parenting destiny of Jason and Imelda, Stella the emotional upsurge accompanying Isabella's arrival on stage. Their pondering was interrupted by lunch boxes containing a vegetable wrap and a cellophaned cookie. The perfunctory enquiry of their choice of beverage was delivered by a miserable young male attendant who seemed to resent this lunch service to 38 E & F. The cabin of Fiji-bound holidaymakers seemed untroubled by the 'why bother with passenger service' attitude of attendants who broke all airborne cabin service speed records to finish their aisle service to optimise their rest time in the forward and aft servery nooks. The near-inaudible public address system, handicapped by a mumbling first officer, failed to render any clear message about the flight and destination metrics.

The airport immigration and customs areas were swamped by a conjunction of three flights disgorging their hordes of sun seekers. The air conditioning was hardly coping. Queued, it seemed for well over an hour, the now sweaty Bonnie and an agitated Stella finally broke into the arrival hall where they were greeted by a placard spelling out a welcome to a Mr and Mrs Bono Stellar. They gently corrected the hotel representative who had run out of welcome garlands. Their bags were rolled out to the resort shuttle already packed with fellow resort participants.

The hotel reception area was in chaos as staff explained to an over flowing garlanded mob that rooms were not ready. An hour later, on their way up to their reef and ocean view room located on the second floor, they noted the building had enjoyed better days. Their jaded verandaed room, with a king-size bed, tiled floors and frayed and faded sun lounges, had its ambience further ruined by both a noisy air conditioner and a thumping overhead fan whose discoloured blades were spotted with insect excreta. They talked about changing rooms but since they were only there for a week so decided not to bother. One next door room was unoccupied while the other had a young Japanese couple in residence.

They skipped the welcoming drinks function by the pool to explore the tropical garden surrounds of the resort. They flinched at the sight of the odd tissue entangled in the undergrowth whilst avoiding being tripped over by the uneven pavers on the pathway. Their choice of dinner venue was the Hideaway restaurant offering select Pacific cuisine. Waiters seem overwhelmed by the demands of diners taking ages before drink and food orders were received and delivered. The steamed reef fish main course sagged coldly against sprigs of unknown wilted green leaves. A disheartened couple returned to their room to make the best of their duty-free wine.

The alcohol, the air journey and stress-induced tiredness dampened any romantic exchange. After showering they fell into bed, and following a cursory cuddle of the geriatric kind, they fell asleep. At 3am they were awakened by fire alarms. A manager came to their door to explain that their Japanese neighbours had set off alarms when they had tried to create a steam room in their bathroom. They had sealed its door and vents with towels and ran hot water in the bath and shower. Bonnie commented to a less impressed and sleepy Stella how genius it was to create a romantic place to enjoy.

Stella awoke to find Bonnie nestling up to her and being thanked for her love and kindness. A tearful Bonnie apologised for the family matters which had generated difficulties and reiterated her joy in sharing a life with Stella. A half-awake Stella was torn. She wanted to tell Bonnie about Isabella. She planned to reveal with the caveat that there will be times when romantic opportunities with others will be encountered and both should not be inhibited to enjoy these moments. If they were open about these events then neither of them should be inhibited knowing that their love and sharing always remained fast. For the moment she held her tongue and allowed Bonnie to lead an early morning love-making.

While lazing on their lounges beside the resort pool, Bonnie, in her containing one piece, could not fail to notice how stunning Stella was in her recently acquired bikini. Stella was privately responding to a text message in which Isabella had wished she could be with Stella to share the tropics. Their poolside relaxing was interrupted by a nearby American family, whose three near-teenage children behaved like pool kamikazes running around their lounges, diving in the pool, and yelling inanities about their attributes. When asked by a young Fijian pool attendant to temper their activity, the eldest child, with no reproach from the parents, told him to go and gather coconuts. The couple left the pool to seek sanctuary of their veranda.

Late afternoon found them lounging on the veranda nattering away, while buoyed by room service cocktails. A sozzled Bonnie then asked Stella what she thought of Isabella. Stella, sensing an opportunity to discuss the blooming relationship, said she was quite taken by her and there had been intimacy during her visits.

Trying to placate a shocked Bonnie, Stella went into monologue mode to rationalise and justify how a breach of trust can be acceptable. There will be times, she argued, when attraction and passion will overwhelm relationship bonds whilst not diminishing her love for Bonnie. And she would not be hurt if Bonnie had the occasional romantic venture. She added that a relationship that is open on such matters will be strengthened.

A tearful Bonnie retreated into the room saying you cannot rationalise deceit. She was racked with jealousy and deeply hurt by the defiling of their trust. A love pledge is a rock-solid bond. And really upsetting was how Isabella, a guest, had overstepped the mark. Totally out of character, Bonnie then went into a pique-laden tirade, saying Imelda and Isabella had spoiled her life. Bonnie was inconsolable and wanted to terminate the holiday and return home. Stella's two-timing had wrecked the relationship. Stella tried to bring calm but an emotional Bonnie was not for turning.

Stella left the room, retreated to an outside bar for a drink while ruing her admission. Bonnie's reaction did not surprise. But the hurt was real and retrieving the situation seemed impossible. When she returned to the room around 10 pm Bonnie was sitting on the veranda staring at a cloudy stormy night denying the moon its rightful glow.

Stella, said she was sorry that the Isabella affair occurred, but she did not regret what had happened. She truly loved Bonnie and hoped she would see that this is not worthy of destroying their partnership. Bonnie remained silent. They retreated to bed.

Bonnie woke at 4am and calmly said to Stella that she could not understand why she had betrayed her. Stella retorted that having relationships outside a partnership do not threaten the commitments they made and neither of them should be shackled by new friendships and what is transacted in such friendships, intimate or otherwise. As far as she was concerned there was no betrayal. Morality injunctions now belonged to centuries past.

The impasse persisted through breakfast and neither yielded their positions. They booked a return flight the next day and spent the remaining day reading and sitting alone by the pool. They took separate meals from the hotel buffet that evening.

Their return flight saw the silent couple nose down in books. The cabin attendant, when serving drinks, failed to propel a polite exchange between them. A chatty lady sitting in their row drew little conversation. Bonnie, the closest, used her reading to shelter her from any possible exchange. She mulled over what would eventuate on their return, was perplexed how she had misjudged what their love pact meant to Stella and could not understand her coolness and rationale when explaining what had transpired with Isabella.

Jason, who collected them from the airport, sensed something was amiss because of their early return and the tenseness in their demeanour. On the drive home his accounting of joy with Carmelita drew muted response from his passengers and the usual upbeat Bonnie was clearly not herself. His news that Isabella was coming to Sydney shortly, to look after Carmelita and allow Imelda to go to hospital for a few days for some gynaecological treatment, did not visibly excite his passengers.

The Drummoyne home was full of unhappiness. Both had difficulty in thinking how, if at all, the relationship could continue. They were sleeping apart and had returned to work.

Bonnie's disconsolation did not diminish when reading, in the lunch room, a magazine item outlining how adult relationships were in upheaval in prosperous, urbanised communities now ringed and swamped by social media, selfishness, and egomania. Conditions, it stated, were ripe for transitory love and a growth in transactional relationships. The incidence of fracturing relationships across all adult age groups was increasing and unrelenting. More concerning, it prompted Bonnie to reflect on her capacity to make a loving relationship work.

Both Stella and Bonnie had experienced the interpersonal atmospherics in the past, when moral and emotional divisions threatened relationships. Bonnie, bruised by Stella's revelations, was not taken by the dismissal that their bond was not diminished by an opportunistic intimacy. She struggled emotionally to disentangle the breaking of the chains of trust, commitment, fidelity, and honour implied in their undertaking. She was in a mulish refusal mood.

Stella, considering the maturity and worldliness Bonnie displayed in their life together, had thought she would not encounter this offensiveness and reproach. She was mistaken in judging what Bonnie construed as a healthy partnership, and wondered whether the coolness would persist or would a retrieval be possible.

RELATIONSHIPS

Paternal and domestic pressures mounted on Jason dealing with the Imelda agenda. Unconcerted, she was also insisting on a move from the apartment to a house. Jason encountered the whole repertoire of Imelda's demand ploys. Kitchen table and pillow talk, cunningly framed as non- negotiable duties around the house and baby care, left a yielding Jason with no counter to the charm directives and found himself in optionless traps.

Surprising to Jason was the number of Imelda's hitherto unknown Filipino female friends who began to call by on weekends. Their socialising left nursemaid Jason adrift. On many Sundays when returning with Carmelita from a walk he would find Imelda entertaining her friends of yesteryear. Feelings of being isolated became accentuated as Imelda's discouragement of Bonnie's visits sharpened. And he wondered how he would cope with Isabella when Imelda went to hospital to have a post-natal treatment.

Clare's world was well apart from Stella's and Jason's as she and Jack embarked on their journey of discovery. The intensifying romance was not disrupted by their discussions on whether to live together. They spent happy weekends together at Clare's or having breaks in the country. Jack's unit, a small bedsitter in a desolate apartment block facing other dreary unit complexes and withered garden surrounds, was unsuitable for housing earnest weekend romancing. No match for a high-rise den overlooking the harbour.

They were continuing their management course. The University's TV ads and web site, chock full of images of glamorous, multi-hued students accompanied by claims of first-class faculty and facilities in a University with world-class ranking of research, teaching, and innovation, were utterly laughable. And their woes with their course continued in the subject, Corporate Governance.

Their subject lecturer, working for a small downtown boutique consultancy, routinely arrived late for class and cruelled his teaching with boastful, inane anonymous anecdotes about governance bungles from his apparent client base. The suggested reading guide and on-line case studies seemed unrelated to what was discussed in class. Worse still he allowed himself to be diverted by a couple of class know-alls who dominated his sessions. Fortunately, they had no group case studies to entangle with a hapless group of class-mates. They were both surprised to receive high grades for a subject that received little effort from them.

The emergent challenge for Clare was a proposal by Jack to share a house together.

Whirling in Stella's mind was to how to resolve the impasse with Bonnie. Unsettling her was the flood of text messages from Isabella expressing her eagerness to get together on her visit to look after Carmelita when Imelda went to hospital.

Bonnie decided to talk to her gay work colleague, Anne, about her situation with Stella. This decision troubled Bonnie who felt relationship troubles should be kept in-house. Anne was quite helpful indicating that she or her partner, on rare occasions, following a party with friends, would link up with another party goer for the rest of the night. In their friendship circle such happenings are accepted as a natural expression of happiness, while stressing that the opportunity to share feelings in an intimate way, is one of life's gifts. Annie said the experiences added much to her life with her partner. An agonised Bonnie, thanked Anne, and went for a walk around the centre to reflect on these observations.

When she returned to the office Anne asked Bonnie to have dinner with her to allow Bonnie to talk through her problem.

Anne's apartment startled Bonnie. The paintings, sculptures and wall coverings imitated the styles of some exotic Asian retreat. Erotic female images were clearly discernible in many of the paintings. The music also echoed an Asian derivation. Anne's partner was away in the country supporting her sick mother.

Sitting back enjoying their wine after a meal, Anne spoke of her past amorous adventures before settling down with a partner. She loved her partner but enjoyed the chance, now and again, to experience the passion of female friends to better ground her emotions and feelings about her partner. Passion and sensuality have many forms, she added, and they inform you how your own partnership could be better fulfilled. And she and her partner occasionally used streaming services to watch both male and female gay porn to extend their love making insights and techniques. Anne spoke of how from these activities she learnt a lot about the importance of the touch and touching in a relationship.

Bonnie had difficulty accepting all this. After all she was anchored by her moral precepts underpinning faithful partnerships.

Anne, to illustrate the importance of touch, asked Bonnie if she would like a massage she perfected when on a health retreat in Thailand with her partner. A reluctant Bonnie gave 'a suppose so' response.

A naked, modesty towelled, and a slightly inebriated Bonnie lay flat on her stomach on a massage table in Anne's spare room. As Anne applied her Thai stroking technique Bonnie entered a new world of sensation. After ten minutes she turned on her side and asked Anne to kiss her. It seemed to Bonnie the kiss lingered for some time before Anne stepped up the intensity of the massage.

Bonnie looked at Anne's bedside clock showing 11.25 pm. Beside her a questioning naked Anne asked how she was travelling. Bonnie agreed that the journey just completed had taken her to a different planet. Anne's angular body, she thought, was not a patch on Stella's. Anne's fingers though, with their wonderful body tapping style, had sent her into another sensual universe.

Farewelling Bonnie Anne said that this encounter should make Bonnie realise that preciousness of a partnership is not destroyed through sharing passion with friends. A confused Bonnie taxied back to Drummoyne at midnight intent to review matters with Stella.

Stella was sitting on the lounge reading when Bonnie entered. Bonnie mentioned she had had a lovely evening and excused herself to shower before retiring. Under the shower Bonnie removed the exotic oil Anne had applied and strangely was excited by the memory of Anne's Thai treatment. She could not believe its effects. After showering and feeling emboldened, a naked Bonnie walked into the lounge room and asked Stella if she was coming to bed soon.

Stella noticed Bonnie's slightly reddened torso and became aroused by the body which had delivered those first urgings. A stirred Stella said yes.

The urgent coupling indicated that the romantic ceasefire had not held. At rest, Bonnie in a return serve, detailed her evening and discussions with Anne. Stella, while surprised, thought a revised Bonnie, on faithfulness and loyalty matters, had turned a new leaf. Bonnie said their relationship was too valuable to be sacrificed over occasions of fleeting passion and excused the rancour over Isabella. But to restore honesty and trust, Bonnie requested that Stella, as she would also do, reveal whenever a temptation is afoot. And if Stella wants an occasional dalliance with Isabella, then that is fine but not in their house.

Bonnie felt she had swallowed her principles but her love for Stella was too important to sacrifice over moments of passion exercised elsewhere.

The Drummoyne couple were aglow the next morning as they prepared for work. They talked about Jason and Clare's situations and agreed to take a short holiday in England to visit some historic gardens. Bonnie, while still feeling unease with her agreement with Stella, simply wanted a clear basis to move on together. Stella, whilst relieved, still had to manoeuvre her understanding with Isabella so that a sense of permanence is never contemplated.

Imelda was in full household command as she prepared for her hospital stay and set schedules for Jason. Carmelita's bassinet had been moved to their bedroom to free a room for Isabella. Jason, ever hoping for a respite, felt the pending absence of Imelda as a blessing, if only albeit for a short period. For both, Carmelita was the easiest baby to manage. She slept to schedule, went through routines of feeding, bathing, and comforting without a fuss and caused no trouble when visitors requested a nurse.

Isabella arrived the day before Imelda's admission. She settled into baby caring effortlessly explaining she had raised younger siblings for her mother. Jason was perplexed by the amount of attention given to her dress when working around the apartment.

Isabella rang Stella agreeing to get together when Jason was able to baby-sit.

The lounge patrons at Ryde Sports Club glanced up when a beauty queen entered their den of household escape. No such glamour had been seen since a rock and roll dazzler performed at an anniversary show some years ago. Glancing did not abate as she greeted another smart looking older woman, who also was stylish and attractive. They sat down and, after ordering drinks, fell into a deep conversation.

Stella traversed the revelation history with Bonnie and their resolution about their partnership's future. Stella had trouble reading Isabella's reactions. Finally, a crest-fallen Isabella cattily responded that she was not going to be some gay courtesan, because she had thought a real, committed partnership was in the offing and added that this clearly was not going to eventuate. Stella stayed her response and sat back thinking how to retrieve something - after all this Filipino pearl still brought excitement and reams of desire. She considered how to keep a link and how to appease.

Stella returned to a theme about sharing intimacy which she had previously traversed with Bonnie. What's wrong Isabella if we can have a great time together whenever travel permits, she added. An unsettled Isabella said she wanted more out of a relationship and clearly, she had misread the signals the two had exchanged over the past months. In a huff and without further comment she distracted the lounge dwellers again, when quickly exiting the lounge leaving Stella contemplating the wine glass sitting on the table.

Jason noted an unhappy Isabella when he left for work the next day.

Returning from the hospital in the evening a disgruntled and downcast Jason was reflecting on Imelda's list of piddling home duties which she gave him as he left her ward. He was fed up with the cascading directions. His Filipino belle was testing his goodwill and generating resentment. And her extra week in hospital did not promise relief. He resolved to seek Isabella's view on Imelda's behaviour.

The apartment was quiet when he entered. The kitchen clock was showing 9.30 pm. Carmelita was asleep. In the dark he saw Isabella slumped on the lounge. He could see that she had been crying but did not ask what had upset her. She reached for her glass of wine and asked how Imelda was.

He first baulked at raising his concerns about his wife. But he saw that she was up for a chat when she sat up and talked about the baby. He noted that that she was dressed casually in some sort of house gown.

He said he loved Imelda but found her demands too trying at times. Isabella, backgrounding a younger Imelda, said that she always had a bossy disposition and encouraged him to pushback and to remind Imelda that they are in an equal partnership.Jason thanked her and retired for the night.

As he showered, he heard the bathroom door open. Isabella cleaned her teeth and left. Jason dried himself and donned his shortie pyjamas. As he passed her room, he heard her crying. He asked if she was okay. Her sobbing intensified and he entered room to see if she needed help. She held out her hand and Jason sat on the bed to comfort her. Jason was distracted from her tear-stained face as the bed covers fell away to reveal Isabella in a NZ themed nightie.

Jason found himself consoling the weeping Isabella who was sitting up in bed. Through her sobs she revealed that she had received some upsetting news from Stella but did not elaborate. To Jason's embarrassment he felt his aroused penis swell as his consoling failed to subdue the distressed Filipino.

It seemed a long time before she got up to go the bathroom and apologised for her outburst. A bemused Jason went to his room and heard Isabella retire to her room. He remained highly disturbed by the sight of the weeping Isabella. Around 4 am he heard Isabella callout and he went to see what was wrong. She beckoned him to sit with her as she felt totally alone and miserable.

At 5am a dozing Jason was still sitting up beside Isabella who was asleep under her covers. She woke and said she was sorry for the drama. An understanding Jason said he was happy to comfort her. A grateful Isabella sat up and quickly slipped her hand under Jason's pants and began to caress his penis. A startled Jason pulled away but she murmured that she wanted distraction from her previous day's unhappy events. A surprised and reluctant Jason could not escape. She removed his pants, lifted her nightie, and rolled on top of him. He quickly found himself pinned under an urging Isabella who manually assisted his insertion and then ground herself into an emotional release. His eyes remained shut and his shuddering hardly registered.

A still stunned Jason received an apology from her. Sex was the best way to overcome and to counter personal distress, she explained. A 'sexploited' Jason, recovered his pants and stumbled back to his bedroom to attend to an awakening Carmelita.

At breakfast an embarrassed, silent Jason faced Isabella who was now nursing Carmelita. She again apologised for last night and advised him to just erase it all from his memory. She added she was completely out of order and her emotional state had caused this embarrassing event.

Jason left for work still trying to understand events of the night. He felt unmoved by her action and, inexplicably, he remained emotionally cold. It was as if the mechanical nature of sex delivered an antidote to relieve her personal crisis. It was beyond his comprehension. He would not be relating the episode to Imelda.

Stella tried to contact Isabella over the following week. No response. It was finished, she thought, but the thought of the radiating and fetching Kiwi boutique owner kept up her hope of rapprochement.

The return of a repaired Imelda and the departure of a dejected Isabella cleared the decks for a retuned Jason to share the command of their Ryde nest. Imelda noted his kickback on her requests and, for the time being, his use of the 'I'll attend to it when I'm ready' retort. Imelda feigned to be helpless in countering the assertive Jason. A different charm offensive would have to be put in play to return to the status quo. After six weeks Imelda realised that Jason was not easy for turning even after a night of pleasure. More and more he was leaving her to organise Carmelita's life.

A happier Jason and Bonnie were more relaxed as their home issues seemed to have been addressed. Clare was exhilarated through the relationship with Jack, whose attention and closeness brought a heightened sense of womanliness. Stella still carried a flame for Isabella who had dropped all communication. Her life with Bonnie moved along and their sharing still brought intimate moments to register in their memory diaries.

YEAR ON

Jack thought that it was his good fortune to have Clare by his side. They lived apart but spent most weekends together. He believed he had unravelled her character. Her confident disposition surprised him when she outlined her personal history. Studying together gave him good insight into her character enabling him to anticipate her mood swings. If anything, his relationship and presence had greatly boosted both her feminine self-image and her interest in modern fashion and style. And he gained also through the positive surge in outlook from having a devoted companion.

Level 15 at Pyrmont filled with laughter as Jack and Clare reviewed an email from the course director of their MBA program, responding to their written complaint that their Professor of Global Business regularly broke into Mandarin when dealing with queries from their fellow Chinese student cohort. He allowed these students to mix English and Chinese in their oral case reports. The haughty director attempted to explain that no student gained an advantage from such actions. Their laughter was brought about by the syntactical errors in the email despite the editing of his Word program.

A deepening relationship had propelled Clare into a state of joyfulness. They resolved to move into together once they found an apartment to lease when Pyrmont expired. Encouraged by Jack, Clare spent more time in attending to her clothes selection which allowed an edgy sexiness to emerge from her slinkiness. Jack, an ardent lover, had driven the sourness out of Clare's outlook on life and turned her face to the sun. Stella could not believe the change in her daughter, believing Jack was a miracle worker.

They had found in the Hunter valley a weekend retreat which they rented periodically for their weekends away. It was haven for rest and intimacy. They used the daytime for walking and sampling the wines of the region. They rued the adverse, intrusive impact in the locality from golf courses and housing estates dotted around the vineyards. Some wineries were off-putting because wine presentations were secondary to food and merchandise sales. Many outlets had the feeling of tawdry bazaars when suffering the onslaught of tourist bus groups.

Their cottage had total privacy. Its bay windows overlooked a vineyard and an outside hot tub sheltered behind a hedged alcove. On warm nights they enjoyed the tub for a chance for naked frolics and inventive foreplay especially on clear moonlit nights. Clare now realised how love in a relationship added so much potency to intimate moments. And Jack's actions had doused any doubt she had about the attractiveness and appeal of her slender figure. He was forever complimenting her vivacity and, when shopping together, he always pointed out underwear he believed suited her svelteness. On many occasions he would draw her attention to images of fashion models he believed could not compare with her.

The relationship helped Clare understand that partnering and coupling were important for surmounting her inner reservations about the importance of others in building a satisfying pathway in life. In the company of Jack it seemed that many of her personal negatives about life were, on reflection, unjustified. And the lovely moments on weekends, when they were nestled down chatting together, she felt a completeness in her well-being never experienced before.

Jack loved to be out and about with Clare. His company sponsored a horse race at a Saturday carnival meeting at Randwick where he and Clare were invited to a special lunch with company executives and their partners. Clare, encouraged by Jack, bought a stylish outfit for the occasion. Stella, who was sent a photo of Clare with Jack at the races, could not believe the transformation of the unfashionable daughter from Homebush. Her earrings were as long as icicles.

The race course, despite heavy recent investment in facilities and stands, struck Clare as the exemplar of awfulness and tacky taste. A venue of despondency, she thought. The cloudy, blustery day meant a knifing wind poured through the canyon of stands, unsettling the crowd as they milled around to view the horses, bought some food and drink, and placed their bets. What surprised her was the elflike height of the jockeys, which was emphasised when they chatted to the owners and trainers during the prerace parade of the horses. Some of the female jockeys looked like pixies poked into riding boots.

Despite the glamour of some women patrons, many of the middle-aged racing crowd generally seemed dour and dowdy. She noticed that there was little jollity in the older crowd chatter, while the drunken raucousness of the younger crowd seemed over the top as well as lowering the tone of the viewing areas. Dress code among the seniors ranged from smart suits and dresses to drab floral dresses, shabby trousers, disarrayed shirts, and ill-fitting blouses. Weirdly, she thought, many men were shod in grimy Nike-like footwear whose soles were about to expire. And the younger brigade, beer and Prosecco infused, cavorted around the outdoor furniture. Lots of the headwear, especially men's logoed caps, seemed hideous. Despite attempts to dress up for the day, many young female patrons, teetering on their high heels, beamed coarseness in their attire made worse by misplaced garish tattoos on their lower and upper limbs.

The dining room was a haven from the cluster of stands, the race mob, and the heavy gusts of the easterly wind. A classy Clare's lively presence and elegance drew attention and compliments from her table companions. She managed to keep a lively conversation going as the group ploughed through crab mousse, braised duck, and eclairs. Jack, proud of her poise and affability, did not mind her taking the limelight through the lunch and it lessened the pain of his losing bets. That evening their love making registered an unusual exquisiteness.

Clare's advent had Jack removing the shroud of divorce and finding himself in a delightful orbit of companionship and romance. He was truly a lucky man given his period of desolation following his divorce. In the past he'd had some terrible days, when he thought of future days alone and without female company. There was a complementarity in their relationship that was difficult to explain. Her boldness counteracted his reservedness. Given their age difference and backgrounds, they had surprisingly gelled. The trans formation of Clare amazed both Bonnie and Stella.

Another surprise landed a week later when Clare announced that she and Jack would be moving mid-year to Brisbane where Jack was taking up a promotion to head his firm's branch office there. They would live together, buy a property, finish their university course on-line and Clare would find a new job. Stella felt this was a positive development and maybe the reformed Clare would finally reach her nirvana there.

The Drummoyne household was busy with preparations for the trip to England. They were taking a direct flight to London. Knowing that British weather can be fickle, their packing covered all eventualities. They invited Jason to housesit while they were away.

Jason gave them an update on Isabella. She had sold her business in Auckland and moved it to Hamilton area where her new partner was living. Her new love interest, Helen, was a prominent female Waikato horse trainer who had regularly patronised her boutique in Auckland. They were living on a horse stud on the outskirts of Matamata. All accounts of their lives claimed that they were a glamorous twosome lighting up the saddling enclosures of North Island racecourses. And their presence at race horse auctions drew attention and comment. A NZ magazine carried a story about their relationship and featured photo shots of the pair in stables modelling new Spring outfits for the forthcoming racing carnivals. The story line revealed that both were very much in love and had found each other at a critical time in their lives. This news bothered Stella at first but she was resigned to not having Isabella on her romance agenda. Bonnie felt a cloud had been removed about Stella and her general happiness moved up several notches.

Home life could not be better Jason reported. A surprisingly calmer and contained Imelda and a lively Carmelita gave him so much joy. They were planning to move to a larger apartment and to have another baby next year. Imelda had an invitation to visit NZ and Isabella would pay for the airfares. Imelda was supplementing their income by doing the odd weekend shift at a new hotel in a nearby business park.

A change in Jason, Bonnie thought, was his assuredness in relationships and concern for the welfare of others. A devoted father he certainly was and his 'taming' of Imelda was an eye-opener. However, she felt Imelda had never warmed to her and limited the opportunities to enjoy grand motherhood. She had deep reservations about Imelda's agendas and feelings. At its base she thought Imelda was a phoney and a master of deceit.

Bonnie thought about this as they winged their way to Heathrow. Their Middle-Eastern carrier had charged extra for their exit row seats which, at least, gave comfort, unlike the tasteless economy meals which had an 'eat me at your own risk' appeal about them. Heathrow airport and immigration were in overdrive now, contending not only with the multitudes from Asia, Americas, and Africa but also the European mobs now outcasts following Britain's detachment from Europe. They reached their London hotel with all their baggage and with the slightest of jet lag and managed to decipher the receptionist's contorted English and gaining entry to their room after three goes with the key card.

Both had been to London before when in their late teens. They noted the dramatic change in the cityscape, the variegated citizenry, and the cleaner and better managed public transport. They speculated which ethnic groups were dominant. In Oxford Street it seemed that that the whole world was represented in the shopping hordes. Their small hotel was near Edgeware Road where the footpaths had become the haunt of middle eastern diners polluting the air with their hookahs. Smoking apparently did not violate local health regulations for venues where food is prepared and served.

They reminisced about their early time times in London, laughing as they recalled the crush in the underground where smoking added to the discomfort from the body odours emanating from the male passengers in their terylene shirts. The mid-afternoon closing of the pubs seemed now ancient history as was the inevitable shroud of smog. There was sadness about the disappearance of tea houses now replaced by coffee, bakery and organic food outlets which had strong continental influences. But somehow, they felt the real loss of Englishness about London. The migrant and visitor throngs, with their foreign accents, habits, and languages, now smothered the cultural earthiness of traditional Londoners which had survived the earlier migrant flows from the Commonwealth.

Time passed quickly and they were soon winging their way home. But within a month the settled family connections were thrown into upheaval. Imelda, who had visited NZ for a week to see Isabella, had returned and informed Jason that she no longer loved him and wanted a divorce. A perplexed and distraught Jason sought reasons, but a cool and steely Imelda simply declared that she had no feelings for him anymore. They would have to come to an arrangement about Carmelita and housing. A tearful Jason could not believe the detached way Imelda delivered all this.

With in a week Jason, now staying with Bonnie and Stella, was in an emotional mess. A distressed and vocally angry Bonnie vented her feelings also and added fuel to the separation bonfire. Stella, despite her counselling and support, could not abate the gloom of mother and son. Jason could not recall anything he had done to bring about this decision of Imelda. He was sure that the event with Isabella was never disclosed to her. All seemed perfect in the household. And the loss of daily connection with Carmelita hurt badly.

Attempts for reconciliation meetings were going nowhere. Imelda, having previously checked the legal provisions of divorce, had handed Jason, when he moved house, a legally drafted schedule which set out the actions both must take to secure the divorce. This premeditation also had dumbfounded Jason and his mother.

To no avail Bonnie thought back to her own marriage to seek an understanding of how a person can suddenly close off all affection for a partner. There were no hints of Imelda's feelings and intentions. It was as if emotions were suddenly guillotined. In Imelda's case it seemed there was a private or hidden agenda for divorce triggered by her yet to be stated plans to start a new life without Jason. It also prompted her to think how a person with this intent could disguise it without alerting a partner.

Stella speculated whether Imelda had consulted Isabella on her intentions. It is was difficult to accept that the charming Imelda could turn into a cold fish. But then again Stella recalled a social researcher's discussion on radio about how some Filipino women can cast a different persona from other women from the Asian region. The theory was that they were shaped somehow by the influential fusion of their Malay, Chinese, Negrito, Spanish, Catholic and American antecedences. A mixture that produced contradictory human values and qualities. They had capacities to quickly switch their 'feeling-dials' from love to anger, hate to respect, generosity to selfishness, demureness to boldness, and submission to dominance and control. Some researchers felt they had an innate coercive psychology. Responding, Bonnie felt this had some plausibility but continued to struggle to understand Imelda's behaviour.

There was no progress on the matrimonial divide despite conversations and visits. Jason struck a stone wall. His solicitor outlined his rights and obligations. The divorce would proceed. The only joy was his times with Carmelita.

He found a boxy bed sit at Gladesville and on occasions he would bring Carmelita to visit Bonnie at Drummoyne.

Try as he might, Jason could not fathom Imelda's behaviour. She indicated repeatedly he was not at fault - she simply had no feeling for him anymore.

Imelda's decision came as a shock to Isabella. Her stay at the horse stud was uneventful and Imelda gave no indication of her position with Jason. Reviewing this news with Helen, Isabella tried to explain Imelda's actions. She always had a remote, steely, inner character which rarely was revealed and her emotional repertoire always seemed stifled, Isabella recounted. Her family in Manilla felt she showed little warmth, a cold fish really, and there was virtually no communication with them after she arrived in Australia. She never returned to Manilla.

NAVIGATING

Jason's and Imelda's solicitors confirmed that, following the family court's decision, the marriage was terminated and the financial and custody arrangements agreed were unexceptional. Both had to build new lives apart. Imelda was now marching forward while Jason was wallowing in misery.

Bonnie reminded Jason, who had hoped that Imelda would change her position before the divorce finalisation, that he had to prepare for intermittent care of Carmelita whilst emotionally detaching himself from Imelda altogether. Jason's state of mind was not in good place and his fragility of character became exposed during his bouts of depression. He managed to hold onto his job, relying on Bonnie's support whenever he needed it during his time with Carmelita. His weight ballooned and whilst never a fashion king, he paid little attention to his appearance. A stranger, observing him shambling in the street, saw a straggly, despondent little man, unshaven with a vacant expression. Stella observed that Jason had seemed to have shrunk in size and was increasingly withdrawn.

Occasional news gave the impression that Imelda was out and about. Carmelita was in day-care whilst Imelda worked as an events manager for a hospitality operator. On the rare occasion their paths crossed, Bonnie noted that Imelda had upped her appearance with a change in hair style and outfits. The changes seemed to counter her petiteness and produced a more earthy look. Jason understood she was occasionally patronising some inner-city Spanish or South American bars in company with a group of male and female friends. During the handover with Carmelita, Imelda never asked Jason how he was faring or what was going on in his life. Her total disinterest in him was reaffirmed.

For Bonnie Jason's separation was hitting hard. She reflected on her own marriage breakup and tried to convey to Jason how he might adjust and get his life back on track. She was sharing his pain and dismay.

Bonnie was also reflecting about how quickly she and Stella were falling into partnership routines. Unnervingly they often found themselves thinking about the same issue and surprised themselves on the large amount of agreement they had on outside social and political controversies. But bubbling under the surface was Bonnie's feeling that there were parts of Stella's character she had yet to unravel. Despite the settlement of the Isabella affair there were still many times she sensed that there was a different Stella yet to make an appearance. Often her too rigid and determined positions on emotional matters were unsettling.

At work Bonnie still revelled in the horticultural collegiality where the age and gender mixture always managed to give joy and friendship. Often, she found herself, during the morning breaks, in the company of Don, one of the new Centre's supervisors. A widower, the 61-year-old had moved down from the Blue Mountains to be close to his grandchildren. Always with a keen sense of humour, Don regaled Bonnie with stories about when he worked in a dysfunctional local council's parks and gardens division where staff spent most of their time driving around in trucks, having multiple drink breaks and smokos, and rarely met a spade, shrub, worm or weed.

Don's thick-set frame, wispish grey hair, weathered face, strong shoulders, and baritone voice seemed to match his demeanour as a dinkum Aussie. He was always ready to see humour in any situation. In the classic open Australian way, Don quickly outlined his life history as well as his troubles finding friendship in Sydney. He admitted he struggled to adjust for many years after the loss of his wife. Work to him was the perfect antidote to loneliness.

The interaction with Don had Bonnie musing what was it about the company of men that conveyed a different frizzante to that of women. Talking to Don alerted her to the strength, boldness and earthiness men possessed while reminding her why she was drawn to manliness. As the weeks unfolded, she surprised herself on how much she looked forward to Don's company. She found his incidental chatter and views of the world, together with perspectives of how he managed his daily affairs, especially refreshing.

Don's maturity, experience and old-world courteous-ness and manners were revealed in his gracious supervision, style especially with sales staff. The doggedness of senior casuals and omissions of junior staff were countered by his polite reminders to respect customers while cautioning staff that they are the public face of the garden centre. He always seemed unflustered by staff, customer, management complaints, which he effortlessly resolved leaving many complainants feeling guilty for raising the them.

Rarely discussed was Bonnie's home life with Stella. Their relationship seemed very natural were the views of centre colleagues. And Don felt as much through their morning chats.

Invitations to a staff-only formal dinner to celebrate the centre's 25th anniversary sat on the morning coffee table. Both Bonnie and Don had accepted. Bonnie, aware that Don had no car, offered to give a ride to the dinner, which was in a restaurant in north-west Sydney. Initially Don indicated he was not intending to go but, at the urging of Bonnie, he had accepted.

Cars pulled up alongside theirs at the myriad of traffic signals, which, together with an epidemic of variable speed zones, plagued Sydney's north west roads. Their drivers would have seen a middle-aged couple in deep, cheerful conversation. The lady driver was in an off-shoulder apricot-coloured dress and the man in a light-coloured blue suit with what seemed a polka-dot bow tie.

The restaurant, with a glassed frontage and roof, nestled within a high-rise cluster of apartments and shops which all faced a floodlit artificial lagoon. The venue harboured the horticultural guests seated around tables displaying profusions of flowers. An outsider could have mistaken it all for a floricultural display in a conservatory. Bonnie was electric with chat as she told table companions about her humorous, historical encounters with customers. The story teller had Don totally engrossed and captivated.

Bonnie and Don took their after-dinner coffee standing together on the terrace facing the lagoon. They agreed that the dinner was great and were lucky to have a job with a fine employer. Alongside Don, Bonnie could feel a romantic twinge sweep over her. This surprised her. The advent of Stella had suspended any interest in males. But standing beside Don reminded her of the kind of emotions associated with being close to a man. And now she used all her will power not to convey too much warmth towards Don.

Outside his house Don thanked Bonnie for the evening and the chauffeuring as well as expressing, as he alighted, his good fortune to have been in her company for a most magical evening. Driving away Bonnie became disturbed by her mix of emotions when juggling feelings about Don and Stella within her moral boundaries. The account of the evening function to Stella mentioned her giving a lift to a fellow employee, Don.

Over the following weeks the emotional struggle did not subside as she felt more and more compelled to spend more time with Don at work.

News from Brisbane generated surprise at Drummoyne. Clare had announced that she and Jack were to marry at year end. The unbelievable had occurred, Stella remarked. Clare also asked Stella and Bonnie to visit Brisbane for a week to celebrate the forthcoming nuptials. Bonnie indicated she needed to support Jason in Sydney and declined.

In Brisbane Stella dined with the wedlock bound. In Drummoyne Bonnie farewelled Jason who collected Carmelita after a Saturday's babysitting. The following morning Bonnie received a phone call from Don who asked whether she was free to help him with some furniture selection at his local shopping mall. Hesitant at first, she agreed to meet up

Weaving through the lounge settings Bonnie kept Don alerted to the pitfalls of various furniture fabrics. A setting was ordered and they decided to take lunch at a nearby Italian restaurant full of young and older patrons of Mediterranean descent.

As they chatted away over their parmigiana servings Bonnie was losing the thread of the conversation as enrapturing pulses overwhelmed her focus. She tried to think through what was it about Don that brought these reactions. Their lunch suffered an unbelievable, reverberating din from fellow diners who, in their traditional Sunday lunch outings, generated a constant wall of noise as families swept through their pizzas and pastas. They quickly finished their meal and Don escorted her to the car park. As he said goodbye Bonnie gave him a kiss on his cheek thanking him for the lunch. Driving home Bonnie felt elated whilst not regretting her action.

Following her week in Brisbane, Stella, arriving back with a pink noose of sunburn around her neck, reported that the happy couple were in seventh heaven in the sunshine state. The big news about Clare was her pregnancy, her happiness and her total transformation in style and outlook. A clearly besotted Jack was over the moon with the prospects of marriage and fatherhood, she added. The photos Stella produced confirmed that the now charming Clare had undergone further glamour transfusion since moving to Brisbane. Bonnie casually mentioned that last Sunday she went to a mall to help Don choose some furniture.

The garden centre, following an advertising blitz in the media, was experiencing record trade. Bonnie, now working full hours, could not believe the pent-up demand for garden products. Don's attentiveness was not diminished by the increased business. From time-to-time little gifts, including chocolates, appeared on her desk with a simple 'please-enjoy' note from Don. Friendship was blossoming and an agitated Bonnie was trying to clear an emotional pathway to resolve what she considered to be her emerging passion dilemma.

After a busy sales promotion Friday a few of the Centre's staff, including Don and Bonnie, went to the local sports club for an after-work drink. Left alone following the departure of colleagues Bonnie gave Don more of her life's history including Jason's divorce and her relationship with Stella. Around 7pm as they walked back arm in arm to her car, Bonnie, though tormented by her dilemma, had decided to vent her feelings to Don. In the shadows of the underground car park Bonnie, overflowing with feeling, turned, and embraced Don. The intensity of the reciprocation of their kisses meant a flame had been lit. Pulling away an apologetic Bonnie bid Don goodnight. He said there was no need to apologise because he too wanted his feelings known.

Over dinner Stella noted that Bonnie seemed unusually chatty as she reviewed her day at work. In bed that night a troubled Bonnie indicated that she was not well and declined Stella's normal Friday night jaunt of an-end-of-week caressing.

The following week Bonnie spent time looking at various on-line references giving both experience accounts and advice on how mature adults, including adulterers and bed-hoppers, have dealt emotionally with a mix of sexual relationships. Surprising her were the reports that many experienced no discomfort in managing intimate moments. Switches in gender posed little difficulty for some. Her quandary with Stella and Don remained.

The garden centre's announcement, that it was merging with other centres in Sydney to grow both wholesale and retail opportunities, took staff by surprise. Part of the merger activity was to require key staff to attend a two-day training workshop at a hotel in Wollongong next month. Training was to focus on the new systems and marketing approaches the merger would adopt. Both Bonnie and Don were on the training list.

PARTNERING

The beachside hotel, overlooking the Pacific Ocean, had a backdrop of closely packed suburbs backed by a hinterland of escarpments and distant ranges. The urban setting and the circulating swish of road traffic depressed the ambience of the hotel's ocean side location. Twenty years of erosive salt-laden breezes, low maintenance standards, together with dated décor, all conspired to produce a haggard looking hotel. The parking garage had an 'out of service' lift and the dump bins overflowed with refuse.

This is no Shangri-La remarked Don as he and Bonnie registered at the reception desk, which had deeply scuffed front veneer panels from years of assault from wayward baggage. The foyer's faded, and worn carpet escaped notice via the faulty lighting. Upstairs the corridors reeked of citrus air-freshener, which wafted out of the guest rooms. All the 30 attendees were assigned escarpment view rooms and received packages of training materials. Over pre dinner drinks they discovered that no one had an ocean view room.

During dinner the program leader, Gilbert (call me Gil), outlined the training agenda. His monotone presentation did not inspire. Unhelpful was his physical appearance - a short, bald, goateed, baggy eyed man, whose prominent stomach threatened to overturn the lectern whenever he moved forward. The trainees were a mix of age and gender. Most were casually dressed with the usual 'denimised' workshop rig. Bonnie was relieved they had not been issued logoed T-shirts and caps for use during the weekend.

Don's room was on the second floor while Bonnie's was on the third. Following a quick drink at the bar with colleagues Bonnie excused herself for an early night. Don remained regaling his drinking group with humorous anecdotes of mismanagement and horticultural horrors, drawn from his jobs with local councils.

After phoning Stella, Bonnie showered and retired for the night. Sleep eluded her as she thought through relationship scenarios with Don and Stella. The desire to get close to Don pressed hard on her heart, while feelings for Stella remained mixed. Waking at 5am, she thought she would use the opportunity at the hotel to test the boundaries of her ardour for Don. if an opportunity arose.

The dismal breakfast was hopefully not an omen for the training day ahead, Bonnie reflected. Breakfast cereal had disgorged over the table from their plastic silos, eggs, bacon, tomatoes, and sausages cooled and wallowed in greasy bain-maries, toast failed to brown properly and the coffee dispenser issued a black liquid imitation of coffee. Escaping the breakfast buffet Don took Bonnie to an oceanside café where they enjoyed croissants and real coffee. Don was taken by Bonnie's bright blouse and smart casual slacks and sandals. She bloomed in the shimmering morning light of their surfside perch.

The training day unfolded with Gil and his assistant, aided by the new CEO, meandering through expositions of their new enterprise's systems and service requirements. 'Whiteboarded' and 'powerpointed' the staff grappled with the logistical and marketing innovations resulting from the merger. At the finish of the day staff were treated to a seafood buffet and were reminded that they had an early start at 8am next day.

While some staff had post dinner drinks in the bar Bonnie and Don went for a walk along the oceanfront. The night was pitch black and they were soon swallowed up in the night as they headed for a distant promontory. A lone star or perhaps a satellite looked down on a couple in a firm passionate embrace. Bonnie was overwhelmed and surprised Don with her lust and vigour. She could not recall ever experiencing such engulfing passion. They returned to the hotel.

The gentleness of their sex did not reflect the depth of the surging and response and the strength of their entangling and grappling. Bonnie clung to Don as her tremoring abated. Her man delivered so much emotion in the sex. She realised how much she missed a man and the irruptive element of male sex. His masculine force overwhelmed. After a while she straddled Don in a couchant position encouraging him to explore her ampleness. He was tearful with joy. Long into the night they chatted animatedly about how ecstatic they felt. At 2 am Bonnie dressed and returned to her room.

Sunday morning saw Bonnie and Don, each drawing back their frayed curtains to look out through the grimy windows at the distant escarpment shrouded in misty rain. The elation of the previous night had not subsided. A life with Don had an imperative written all over it as Bonnie's thoughts raced through how she would sort out her relationships. The advent of Don had propelled her into an unbounded and strangely welcoming euphoria.

Downstairs, Don, reflecting on her pliant nakedness, understood the issues both would face if they proceeded to an intimate alliance. As he showered, he could not curb thoughts of the passion and willingness conveyed in their interactions. At their first meetings he could never believe that their relationship would lead to the emotional intensity such as that experienced last night. He was simply taken by her inner and outer beauty.

By midafternoon the training was concluded and the CEO thanked the group and emphasised the successes the merger would deliver.

Before leaving Don and Bonnie sat in the hotel bar to consider the future. The pathway forward for Don was uncomplicated. He was prepared to share a life if possible. Bonnie wrestled with the approach to Stella and the consequences of severing their relationship. Last night remained unmelted in her mind. They agreed they would give a month or so to step back, giving Bonnie time to resolve her position. Don said he would accept whatever emerged and which provided the least trauma for her and her family.

Over the next five weeks, at work and at home, Bonnie had the infidelity rattle around in her mind. The tensions, between what the heart signalled and the roadblocks of morality, loyalty, honesty, and honour, were palpable.

An opportunity with Stella for a face to face on the matter arose when Stella began talking enthusiastically about life styles in Brisbane. Surprisingly Stella floated ideas about moving closer to Clare to help with the baby, making money by selling Drummoyne and buying in Brisbane where, also, they could pick up a better paying job.

Bonnie at first did not react thinking about obligations and support for Jason. The Brisbane speculation reminded Bonnie that Stella is not shy in assuming her interests often have primacy.

Feeling squeezed and trapped, she decided it was time to bite the bullet by telling Stella her intention to leave and take up a life with Don. Bonnie pointed out their relationship had travelled its course and that they both should move onto a new life while their age and health were on their side.

Tension permeated their lounge room as a tearful, sorrowful Bonnie and an anger-brewing Stella verbally criss-crossed their views and sentiments.

Stella's sharp retorts focussed on the hurt of separation. Your sorrowfulness does not cancel the misery you have delivered to me, Stella piercingly put. Bonnie had Stella fuming further when she observed that she never regretted them coming together. More wrath was generated when Bonnie said everyone must turn a new page when the next chapter offers so much more. Gaining some boldness Bonnie observed that she had Don, Jason, and Carmelita while Stella had Brisbane, Clare, Jack and soon would be a grandmother. An infuriated Stella left the room, packed some clothes, and left the house with not a further word.

Within three months their Drummoyne house was put on the market, and both had finalised legal matters on the respective share of money from its sale. Stella took leave from work to apartment hunt in Brisbane and Bonnie reviewed housing options with Don.

A bemused Clare and an even more bemused Jason, neither of whom had an inkling of the break up, were not too surprised when news broke.

Don, a happy recipient of the separation, was in high spirits as the prospect of a life with Bonnie became imminent. The stories about the mysterious ways of how love unfolds, were apt, he reflected. While he should pinch himself for his good fortune, Don somehow convinced himself that he and Bonnie were always destined to partner. He shared also the stress Bonnie was undergoing. And he comforted her as she read Stella's bitter text messages, strewn with resentment and hate.

As she prepared the house for sale Bonnie reflected on Stella's reactions whilst retrieving the lovely moments they enjoyed in the house. Her decision to separate seemed now to be right, once she thought through how different her emotional and sensual responses were with Don. It was at a level and intensity never experienced with Stella and her husband. She understood Stella's bitterness but overwhelmingly she saw Don as a partner, where there was to be a sharing of a never-ending journey of love to unfold. And in a strange way she thought that Stella would quickly adjust and put her life back on track.

For Don, partnering again meant his journey towards retirement and life beyond would dispel his deep fear of spending his senior years without a mate and companion - a prospect that often dimmed his sunny outlook. The positive reception to Bonnie from his family brought more joy to his heart.

Trawling through the real estate websites and visiting open houses had Don and Bonnie contending with a house market, which challenged most wallets. Pooling their resources, they felt confident to buy a home close to work, in an area which now had a largely east Asian demographic.

A successful offer on a small brick bungalow, a ten-minute walk from work, galvanised legal action not only to settle the proceeds from the sale of Drummoyne but also the legal arrangements for Don and Bonnie to protect their individual rights as partners in the bungalow.

A dismal Jason had visited their suburb. He noted that their locality had expensive cars nesting on driveways, shops with a proliferation of Asian produce, and lots of elderly folks pounding the footpaths. He saw that neighbourhood backyards had embraced horticulture, imprisoned finches and parrots, and resounded with the woofing and yapping of impounded hounds and terriers. There was the occasional the smell of garlic wafting in the breeze, when he took Carmelita for walks around Bonnie's new neighbourhood.

A busy month had the new partners pushed to their energy and organisational limits. Apart from house movements and setup, they faced work changes, where Bonnie took up a supervisory position and Don took a management job at another Centre. Unsurprisingly Don managed the transitions, eased into homelife and was untroubled handling the new roles of companionship, housemate, and lover. He was the perfect host when they threw a house-warming party with work colleagues during which they heard that their nicknames at work were 'the Bondons'. An inebriated colleague said that they were bound to bond.

Bonnie could not believe her life's journey - a wife, mother, grandmother, divorcee, single parent, gay lover, and now a partner. The joy with Don eclipsed other relationship moments in her life. She worshipped him and he worshipped her- that is what it felt deep down. And now they needed to deepen their bonds and secure the dividends of a shared life. The future of a forlorn Jason weighed heavily on her mind, as did the kind of life Carmelita faced.

Don's children and Sydney relatives greeted Bonnie warmly. His sister, two years older than Don, hosted a barbecue lunch for Bonnie and Don to introduce members of his family. A long afternoon of feasting, banter, and merriment together with anecdotes about Don's early life, had Bonnie feeling that she was a permanent fixture in his family.

Communication with Stella had been confined to legal matters. In Brisbane, Stella had acquired an apartment on the river and had a new job.

Despite close questioning from Clare, Stella did not reveal the break-up background and details apart from a brief outline of Bonnie's involvement with Don. She masked her fury, acrimony, and outrage.

The indented harbour of Sydney and the flood-prone rivered Brisbane produce different geographies to experience. Culturally both cities share a colonial settlement and indigenous displacement periods as well as hosting centuries of immigration. But there were some cultural ambiences afoot in 21st century Brisbane which set it aside from Sydney.

Stella, in her Indooroopilly apartment block and North Quay office building, was quick to notice some Queensland quirkiness. Apart from the drawling enunciation of some, other striking differences were detected among the inhabitants. In her interactions, she encountered more types of the brashly conservative, the defensively insular, the shallowly sophisticated, the unexpectedly naïve, and the irrationally judgemental. Work colleagues from southern states had drawn similar conclusions, adding that there was unwarranted conceit and cockiness amongst these Queenslanders. But Stella, set to establish herself, did not dwell on these irritants as she pushed on to build relationships with Clare and to explore social life.

Her early forays into the after-work drink gatherings and cocktail bar visits, while great for work and social relations, did not unearth companiable prospects. But fate delivered.

She had befriended a city pharmacist when taking her regular Sunday walk. And soon they became part of the regular Sunday walking parade along the riverside paths. Fiona, the consummate professional in the pharmacy, drew Stella's attention by her vitality and engaging personality. When walking the 49-year-old exuded youthfulness, athleticism, and a soft coquettishness. Her strong body was revealed in her sporty walking outfits. Stella was taken by her aerodynamic body, squarish face, piercing blue eyes, boyishly-styled, short-cropped blonde hair, and sturdy legs.

Within a month Stella learnt that Fiona had eschewed marriage, giving life-long support to her widowed father and to run a busy inner-city pharmacy. Well-travelled and committed to feminist politics, Fiona had continually championed women's causes right from her university days. She had flirted with Labor and Green politics but their muddling policies, on small business issues and their indifferences to the need for supporting entrepreneurial activity, pushed her politically to become a fiercely independent advocate in pursuing business justice and fairness agendas. And her hobby of cultivating tropical exotic palms became the focus of their chatter on many Sunday walks.

An invite to spend a Sunday afternoon at Fiona's home hoisted Stella's romantic antenna.

The amazing pattern and structure of palm leaves had Stella intrigued, as they walked through Fiona's micro palm plantation, adjoining her Moggill house. Her 87-year-old, wheel-chaired father, relaxing on the veranda, had met Stella before, sharing afternoon tea with them. Stella had travelled out after her walk and, now amongst the palms, was transfixed by the green coolness. But this did not hinder her attention to Fiona whose long cotton print dress failed to camouflage the firm, vibrant and pressing body within, amplified by her swerving around the palms like a matador. Stella was plagued by the urge to touch Fiona to sense the possibility of any reciprocating electricity.

After dinner, with the father retired for the night, the two were sitting in the dark on a swing lounge on the veranda, drinking, talking, and taking in the blazing starry night. Stella did not flinch when she found a nervous arm around her shoulder pulling her towards Fiona. A not so startled Stella, could not believe how the approach seemed to echo someone with little exposure to romantic overtures. However, progress quickly halted when her father's coughing drifted onto the veranda managing to separate a tentative but potentially amorous clinch.

The following weeks saw the pair spending Sundays together, but with a hesitant sensuality holding them back from expressing deep feelings. Both sketchily outlined their relationship history which revealed that Fiona had never married nor had children. Apparently, a lot of time was devoted to supporting her father and running the business. Stella sensed that Fiona had no serious love affairs and proceeded cautiously to advance her feelings.

As the weeks pressed on, Stella could see that there was a reluctance by Fiona to move past cursory embracing when in private. In her movement and reactions, she felt that Fiona did not appear have the language to express her feelings which, together with her hand and body movements, reflected intimacy inexperience. On Sundays when having coffee in Stella's apartment, Fiona always seemed highly anxious about the occasional embrace that took place. On reflection Stella felt as if Fiona was on her first dating experience. Despite her romantic inhibitions, Fiona delivered a warm and intelligent friendship which removed Stella's anxiety of establishing a new abode in a new city and building a social life.

Exhibition week in Brisbane delivered a long weekend break for locals. On a whim Stella asked Fiona if she could get away for a break to share a villa in a bayside resort, to relax and to enjoy the water. Fiona at first said she could not leave her father but a week later she accepted after one of her father's sisters was to stay with him over the exhibition week.

The two-bedroom villa sat high above the bay looking east. It had a jacuzzi, plunge pool, an extensive lounge area and balcony overlooking the water. The downside was the noise from endless movement of speedboats and music from pleasure and party boats. Fiona arrived on Saturday night after closing her pharmacy.

Stella, uncertain how their sharing would unfold, had prepared a light dinner, and had laid in some champagne to kick start the weekend and perhaps bring Fiona to a more relaxed state. After changing her work clothes and showering, a mildly flushing Fiona joined Stella on the balcony to welcome the evening shadows and moonrise. Her bare-shouldered swing midi-dress was totally becoming. Her radiance transmitted by her movement had Stella quickly confirming her early impressions of her physical beauty. She simply stunned Stella.

After dinner they walked hand in hand in the bayside park not allowing their chatting and mood to be derailed by the smell of diesel fuel, barbecues and kitchen exhausts escaping the moored vessels. The warm humid night closed in on to the two. Stella, attempting to override Fiona's romantic conservatism, talked about the closeness of her past love involvements with women, pointing out how much it uplifted her life and delivered a deep emotional satisfaction which had previously eluded her. Fiona encouraged her to talk further including her views about female love. This was heartening to Stella but little came forth from Fiona.

Back in the lounge Stella's talking about themes of love and relationship continued to dominate. They sat tightly together with Fiona's head resting on Stella's shoulder.

Sitting up in bed the next morning Stella tried to dismiss thoughts of conquest as she looked across at a naked sleeping Fiona. The master and pupil had completed the lesson. A quick learner Stella thought, as she recalled how energised her pupil was. Her conservatism and hesitancy evaporated once their journey was well underway. Fiona's tautness and compactness caught Stella by surprise.

Fiona returned from the bathroom offering Stella a glass of water. Silent at first, Fiona slowly unwound as she nestled against Stella. The night was a total revelation if Stella was to believe what Fiona recounted. The convergence of emotions and reactions had promoted a sexual collision she could not believe was possible. The intertwining of the physical and the emotional had transported Fiona to a hitherto unknown orbit of love. Love declarations flowed. The perky pharmacist had her dose of love potion.

Over the next two days the time with Fiona had restored Stella's spirits through the possibility of a long partnership in the offing. The Jacuzzi had rid Fiona's inhibitions about nudity. She enjoyed mutual massaging and the presence of an ardent lover. They discussed living together but Fiona, because of her commitment to her father, saw that this could be a challenge and subject to what unfolds with his health.

A restored Stella told Clare about her friendship with Fiona. Pregnancy, marriage plans and household affairs weighed heavily on Clare, who, to Stella's surprise, simply complimented her for moving on with her life.

A month later as the sun set in Stella's local park, a celebrant concluded a marriage ceremony for a very pregnant Clare and a beaming Jack. The glamorous guests, Stella and Fiona, gave a toast to the husband and wife. Clare's cordiality and Fiona's graciousness made Stella happy. The four celebrated further at a nearby restaurant. There a confused fusion of Mediterranean and Asian cuisine, a staff of mixed ethnicity, and strangled-piped music struggled to give the restaurant a celebratory ambience.

In Sydney a dispirited Jason digested the news about Clare and Stella, and even the good tidings about his mother did not bring cheer. Imelda's indifference and coldness, as well as her social forays and her reported dating companions only pushed more gloom on his shoulders. His fortnightly tending to Carmelita temporarily raised his spirits, but Sunday evenings, after returning her, always presented him with another period of lonesomeness. He struggled to meet women. Dating ended disappointingly once his responsibility for Carmelita became known. And he continued to agonise about how much he had misjudged Imelda. He now considered her to be totally self-centred and selfish with no semblance of care and kindness towards him and Bonnie.

LOVE WILL OUT

It seemed ages since news had filtered down to Bonnie that the Queensland newlyweds had produced a baby daughter and that Stella had bought a house at Kenmore to be near her new friend, Fiona. Through Jason, who kept an irregular link with Clare after sending her a gift for her baby, she learnt that the two couples were enjoying the bounties of Brisbane life.

Bonnie discussed with Don whether she should reach out to Stella to see whether there was any interest in reconnecting. Don reminded her about the bitterness that flowed and doubted whether the passing of time had changed Stella's disposition.

They enjoyed their neighbourhood. Their close neighbours were welcoming and regularly plied them with garden produce, occasional cakes, and dinner invitations. On one side was a Chinese family from Hong Kong who were zealous gardeners and on the other an uninquisitive widow, a retired chef, who had worked for major Sydney hotels. Neighbours appreciated the gifts of pot plants Bonnnie provided them occasionally from the dispersal stock of the Centre. And Don gave them lots of tips on plant selection and cultivation.

To celebrate an anniversary of their first meeting they had decided to take an Asian ocean cruise sometime at the end of Autumn.

Sitting on the back porch of their bungalow, Bonnie scanned through a cruise ship brochure Don had supplied before he went interstate on a week's work assignment.

They were encouraged by his neighbours to go visit their corner of the world. Reading the blurb accompanying various the ship's feature photos Bonnie felt she was being swamped by an adjectival blitz. The ship had an asymmetrical layout, provided immersive experiences, offered a myriad of itineraries, allowed Asian cultural nuances, supplied convivial atmosphere, gave onboard sensory stimulation on sea days, assured fine cuisine, employed sustainable and ethical practices, and included a personalised valet for your indulgence. Child passengers were verboten.

How sweet it was that Don wanted to celebrate this way, Bonnie thought. A romantic voyage whilst exploring exotic Asian locations felt right. A kind of love pilgrimage maybe. Looking at the brochure photos she thought that a bit of attention to her wardrobe might be on the cards, if to match the cavorting, champagning, and chomping sophisticates pictured in the brochure.

Although Don was only absent a week, she sorely missed his presence. Their adjustments to life together rarely encountered any real hiccups. Their jobs were rostered five days together through a seven-day period, so they had opportunities to avoid weekend leisure crowds. Their major enjoyment was bushwalking where Don's knowledge of native flora and fauna continually impressed.

Bonnie remained concerned about Jason's welfare and outlook. While there were signs that he had moved on from Imelda in his emotional agenda, he nevertheless appeared to be stuck in a relationship quagmire where companionship seemed unreachable. Downcast was his constant condition.

An alert Bonnie, however, saw an opportunity to match-make when she met her Chinese neighbour's only daughter, who had arrived recently from Hong Kong after her divorce following a six-year marriage with an

English architect. The daughter told Bonnie that the new government regime in Hong Kong had propelled her friends and work colleagues to leave, while entry visas to Australia were readily issued.

Bonnie found their 31-year-old daughter, Lucy, had an engaging personality which was not hindered by her soft voice and quiet, polite demeanour. Her slightness did not suggest any frailness. Unemployed she spent time assisting parents with their chores and pursuing her pen drawing hobby. The absence of shyness meant that she was always prepared to have a prolonged chat whenever they met.

One Sunday, when it was not Jason's turn with Carmelita, Bonnie invited their neighbours in for a barbecue lunch. Don, who had mastered the techniques using charcoal to cook the beef, was keen to display his culinary skills and was the buoyant, funny host. Lucy and her parents and the widow next door were invitees. A nervous Bonnie watched how Jason joined in and was relieved that he had struck up a conversation with Lucy whom he was impressing with his knowledge of Chinese cinema.

It seemed that months had passed before Lucy's parents invited them back for a dinner including an invitation to Jason. Following the dinner Lucy spent time with Jason discussing how the China had many regional languages which were still used despite the compulsion for citizens to adopt Mandarin as the official language. Shortly after that they were invited to a birthday party for Lucy's father.

A happier Jason sought Bonnie's advice on how he might approach Lucy to accompany him to an exhibition on Chinese cinematography. Following enquiries with Chinese customers, Bonnie invited Lucy for coffee at the Centre's café and arranged for Jason to attend. On the pretence of an office commitment Bonnie would leave her alone with

Jason. A buoyed Jason rang Bonnie to let her know that Lucy had accepted his invite.

At the exhibition hall, while having lunch in its bistro, Jason and Lucy exchanged brief stories of their lives. Lucy was childless. Her husband all but abandoned her because of his travel for work. Her former job in a bank kept her linked with friends and was her main social outlet. Jason skimmed over his life with Imelda outlining his present parental obligations and the support from Bonnie.

Their relationship moved at snail's pace, affected by cultural inhibitions and their apprehensiveness about close involvement. Carmelita was not an impediment, Jason had gathered. Relationship building will be a challenge, Jason thought. Certainly, he would be vigilant when discussing personal matters and inner sentiments.

Lucy had hinted that she would like to experience the outback, given her life in the urban crush of Hong Kong. Jason suggested that they take a week-long bus tour to Broken Hill in western NSW. They could travel together and book single accommodation. The tour was booked and six weeks later saw them underway.

In a roadside café at Bathurst, an animated Lucy expressed her wonder about the Blue Mountains and was struck by the geological formations and vegetation she saw on the ascent and descent. Jason, heartened by her enjoyment of the trip, felt that Lucy was warming to him. As they rejoined their bus group, he noted her slimness did not affect her femininity which was enhanced by her tight slim-fit jeans.

Their Dubbo motel, Jack 'n' Roo Inn, was prematurely aged through poor construction and inadequate upkeep of its public areas. The 23 bus travellers slotted into their rooms; Jason had a ground floor disabled unit and Lucy an upper-level unit facing the highway. After dinner they walked/talked the town centre, managing to avoid being impaled by electrically-powered youths scootering and skateboarding the footpaths. Before retiring to her unit Lucy thanked Jason for organising the trip. The faintest of a glancing kiss on his cheek drew Jason's night to a close.

Westward bound, the landscape gradually lost vegetation cover. Cattle, goats, sheep, emus, and kangaroos, uninhibited by the flawed fencing, competed for the sparse greenery. Not a rabbit was sighted. Lucy marvelled at the distances between towns. She was entertained at bus rest stops by the speed of fellow travellers alighting the bus to answer the call of nature. The bus driver's humour and dry wit kept the tour group jolly and friendly. Jason's nerviness about Lucy faded as their conversation deepened and as their personal histories unfolded in the long travel stretches of their west bound bus.

Broken Hill's townscape, infected by its mining history, was calling out for decent coats of paint to enliven its buildings. Its urban clusters, hedged in by arid terrain, housed its miners, service personnel and retirees. The tour quickly provided Jason and Lucy the highpoints of Broken Hill's cultural, civic, and industrial life. The city gave Jason a feeling that it was just clinging to life and its mining arteries were in danger off giving up the ghost. She was intrigued by its history and its endeavours to further the creative arts. She was also amused by their motel, The Tuckbox. Many guests left their boots outside their unit doors and the parking area was dotted with vehicles encrusted with red dirt. She did not understand why, when booking in, the motel manager asked her whether she wanted milk. After dinner Lucy joined Jason in his room to watch some TV.

Jason could not get a real sense of Lucy's feeling towards him. Her amiableness, chattiness and spirited conversation was a positive pointer but, whilst sitting together, he felt there was little overt display or suggestion of affection. As she left to go to her room, wary of offending her, he withheld a goodnight kiss. Her timidity or modesty shone like a beacon and he was anxious not to be too forward and wrecking a budding relationship.

Their return trip took them to Orange, their last stop, where they visited a nearby gold mine. They did not join the group for dinner preferring to visit a nearby arcade which had a food court with a surprising variety of Asian buffets. As they walked back to their motel Jason sensed a mood change in Lucy who was quite animated in her chat while holding onto his left arm. Back in his room preparing a drink of tea, Jason found Lucy standing behind him with her arms wrapped around his chest.

When they finished their drink Lucy thanked Jason for the trip and his generosity in meeting their costs. For the first time she talked in detail of a former marriage revealing the attrition of love and her husband's disinterest in her welfare and needs. Towards the end of her marriage, she discovered that he was having extra-marital relationships with men in Bangkok and Manilla. Jason found a weeping Lucy nestling up to him. This emotional reaction surprised Jason but signalled a different Lucy was being unveiled.

There is a sweetness in her revelation, Jason thought. He kissed her forehead and handed her a tissue to dry her eyes.

A short, hesitant exchange of a kiss seemed a natural progression after this disclosure of her past. Her thin lips conveyed little sensuality to a now encouraged Jason. As they embraced her slenderness became very apparent. Disengaging and before retiring to her room, Lucy indicated that she liked Jason very much and hoped they could continue their friendship when back in Sydney. The short embrace had rekindled Jason's heart.

House sitter Jason settled into Bonnie's house and looked forward to the four weeks of comfort as the cruising couple plied the Asian seas and experienced the Orient. Lucy and her mother delivered treats and the odd dinner for Jason. Occasionally Lucy would call in to share some innocent TV viewing.

In his third house-sitting week Lucy mentioned that her parents were away next long weekend celebrating their cousin's birthday in Brisbane. She invited Jason to join her for an evening meal on Saturday night.

Jason could not believe the Lucy who greeted him at the door. A transformation had occurred. Her beautiful pink and black cheongsam stunned Jason, as did her swept hairstyle which framed a face enlivened by imposing eye and lip cosmetics.

The Hong Kong belle escorted Jason to the lounge room where they toasted each other with the non-alcoholic wine Jason had brought. Dinner followed, where Jason had trouble finding words to compliment Lucy for the sumptuous meal they enjoyed. As the clock struck 11pm the feasted couple sat back in the lounge to enjoy some tea. Jason edged into conversation which might give him a clue whether their relationship had prospect for a deeper commitment.

Returning home at midnight Jason remained unclear where their friendship was heading. The prolonged goodnight kiss carried some hopeful sign.

On Sunday morning he received a phone call from Lucy who was having difficulty with the electricity supply. Barefooted she greeted him at the door wearing a garment which seemed to him to be a cross between a short-sleeve housecoat and a knee-length dressing gown. He reset the tripped fuse in the meter box and restored power. They retired to the back porch where Lucy served him coffee. In the sun he was again taken by her pearly delicate skin. As they chatted Jason kept wondering whether he should be bold and somehow advance their friendship.

Lucy revealed that her hobby was pen and ink drawing especially faces of friends and strangers. She invited him to come into her small study where she produced and kept her drawings. Two sketches of Jason were included in her portfolio. As he looked over her shoulder at what were his unflattering face portrayals, he kissed her on the neck. Pulling away Lucy placed the portfolio on her desk. In what seemed ages she approached Jason, wrapped her arms around his head, encouraging him into a responding kiss exchange.

Pausing they sat down on her studio settee where waveringly she explained that, aside from her former husband, she had never been close to a man. Jason indicated he understood what she meant. They sat together for a while exploring aspects of romantic relationships and what they each expected from such relationships. Jolting Jason, she said if Jason was comfortable, she would like to make love with him. She would come to his house tonight because, he guessed, she did want to sully her respect for her parents and their home. His smile and assenting embrace signalled a keenness to participate.

All Sunday afternoon Jason tried to untangle the motives for this abrupt and unexpected request of Lucy.

Sunday night the nervous couple entered Jason's recently hoovered bedroom. Fresh sheets covered the bed which, to Lucy's surprise, swarmed with pillows. The dim light did not hide the sheen on her body as she sat back naked on his bed. The now experienced Jason was quick to claim his prize. The initial tentativeness was gone, overtaken by the lightness and quietness of her yielding leaving Jason elated but somewhat stunned. His silent lover, now lying beside him, signalled her joy through her intense clasping of his body. When she spoke, she said she never thought that she would ever again have another opportunity to feel another man's heart.

Keen to discover what the future promised Jason found that Lucy was eager to continue their association. Both reflected, in their ensuing conversations, that both had experienced long periods of being lonely and yearned for the kind of connection produced through a deep loving friendship.

The following weeks were revelatory. Lucy and Jason had told parents that they were close friends and, to Jason's delight, Lucy warmed to Carmelita. And this eased his concerns now the divorce conditions and access arrangements had been finalised. They quickly formed a dating routine and when possible, Lucy would pay an evening visit to Jason's bed-sit.

Friends and family were buffeted by Bonnie's cruise stories, including the various escapades of Don. Don starred. Their trivia team were successful through his knowledge of current affairs, plants, and animals and he had wins at the shipboard deck games. Many of the excursions disappointed or were expensive so Don hired taxis to explore other ports of call. He was the master in negotiating fares and bargaining prices in shops. And somehow, he wangled a deluxe suite upgrade because they encountered endless plumbing malfunctions in the bathroom. The downside of the cruise was the marshalling of passengers for land-based excursions where they felt they were herded and treated like goats. Bonnie sympathised with the plight of the crew who seemed to have never ending daily duties and who spent a good portion of the year at sea away from family.

A popular morning TV chat show had Bonnie intrigued. The female host was interviewing two women about relationships amongst mature women. There was a culture expert and a therapist. Topics of focus included explanations of why there was seemingly a spate of older women leaving long established heterosexual partnerships and setting up new lives with female partners. Many explanations were offered. The culture expert focussed on community acceptance of diverse gender relationships which made same-sex partnerships more socially and widely acceptable. The therapist argued that older woman sought the possibility of deeper, emotional, and sensual connection and the compassion offered by other women.

A mature Bonnie reflected on her partnership history. While agreeing with most of the interview observations, she always had a feeling that she had an innate drive to have a male as a mate and confidant. She did not regret her past decisions, but if she was honest, she always found something unsettling with life with Stella. And after she encountered Don, she experienced an increasing emotional unease with Stella.

Bonnie was readily swept into Don's extended family and found herself spending a lot of social time with his older sister and her girlfriends. Here she was exposed to ladies' lunches, theatre visits and outlet shopping. The sister had never-ending insights into what constituted the good life, reinforcing the adage that we are here in the world to live not to just simply exist. What amused her was the openness of the friendship group in talking frankly about intimate moments in their family lives. Nothing was off limits leaving Bonnie feeling that perhaps her reluctance to disclose aspects of her private life, meant she was the odd one in the group.

Life with Don was untroubled and she marvelled at his capacity to anticipate her moods and feelings. He moved easily between the world of work, home life and his relatives, quickly resolving problems that arose.

MANY YEARS ON

Bonnie and Don are well retired. Don retains a connection with work through contract logistical work. Arthritis plagues Don and Bonnie accepts her plumper figure. Contact with granddaughter Carmelita is sporadic, since Imelda has moved to Canberra to join her new husband, a retired army officer. They are running a home catering business which limits journeys to Sydney. Jason is a regular visitor normally accompanied by Lucy, who visits her parents next door. Carmelita stays with Bonnie whenever she is visiting on her school holidays.

Bonnie rarely hears news about Brisbane and her links with Stella and Clare are finished. Through Jason she knows that Stella has a partner, Fiona, and that Jack and Clare have a daughter and are well settled into family life. Life with Don rarely encountered setbacks. Every day she thinks of her good fortune to have Don beside her. Memories from an exciting holiday in the South Island of New Zealand linger as Bonnie and Don set about renovations of their inner-west bungalow.

Their Kiwi sojourn in late October rekindled their interest in the decorative power of flowers and trees. Their floral senses were overwhelmed by the flourishing South Island gardens encouraged by a warmish Spring. Many backyards in the townships seemed veritable market gardens. The landform and treescape variation never failed to impress. And the orchard blossoms were outstanding.

As they travelled around thoughts about New Zealander, Stella, occasionally emerged. They were continually surprised about the bonhomie they struck when chatting to the locals, who seemed imbued with an everlasting sunny outlook. When talking to the locals in the far south, they found accents tough to grasp. Don often struggled to understand the odd word. In the town of Gore they had a hilarious time with a waitress as they reclarified their food orders. Words like 'Bach', 'joker', 'sparrow fart', 'biff', and the phrase 'a kick in the guts' were additions to his vocabulary. And he was surprised that the towelling hat retained its appeal with many of the rural menfolk.

The coastal, riverine and mountain terrains delivered scenic bonuses. It seemed the uplifted landscape mirrored the uplifted spirit of the Kiwis encountered on their travels. One special evening they stayed in a chalet unit with a distant view of the iconic Mount Cook. Never retiring on romantic matters Don encouraged Bonnie to join him in their jacuzzi with a great outlook to the mountain. The jacuzzi, the sparkling pinot, the emboldened naked frolicking generated an adventurous night of love making. Mature love saluted the snow-topped mountain.

They were both struck by the dominant place of Māori affairs of the country. News reports featured Maori issues regularly. They had obvious political clout which attracted critical comment about their insistence on their rights and entitlements. One Otago farmer, jaundiced by Māori dominance, told Don that the land of the long white cloud had turned into the land of the long black cloud. It prompted Don to muse about how much further Indigenous causes in Australia had still to travel before they reached the position of Māori, politically and economically.

Their final days in New Zealand were spent in and around Christchurch. On the last day, they visited the stunning Banks peninsula with its Maori and French histories and its wonderful harbour. This capped a treat- laden holiday and both were surprised what a hidden treasure the South Island was. The remnant wreckage and legacies from the devastating Christchurch earthquake did not offset their spirits as they passed its iconic parks and home gardens on the way to the airport.

Bonnie's sadness about the limited contact with Carmelita was somewhat countered by her joy from Jason's relationship with Lucy which was going from strength to strength. Unclear was the view of Lucy's parents about their daughter's involvement with Jason. Bonnie sensed a less than enthusiastic reaction from Lucy's father. His interaction with Jason seemed distant rarely joining in the conversation when they were all together. In private conversations with Lucy's mother Bonnie sensed that she was delighted that her daughter had a loving friendship.

Life for Jason and Lucy had gone well for the four years since they had started living together in Jason's new apartment. Lucy at first took her time to adjust to partnering life. In her quiet way she grew in persuasive skills. She quickly found that Jason reacted well to her growing confidence and initiative in domestic matters. Unlike life with Imelda, Jason experienced warmth and honesty with Lucy and their closer moments delivered delight. Lucy, despite her disappointing experience in marriage, extended the boundaries in love-making finding ways to keep Jason's coupling interest alive. After many discussions they had agreed not to have children, a position they had yet to reveal to their parents. Lucy had enjoyed the status of aunt during Carmelita's visits.

Apartment life no longer irritated Jason, as Lucy turned her well-honed decorating skills from high-rise life in Hong Kong to produce a softly-furnished ambience, with wall hangings full of Chinese and Australian themes. Their fourth-floor balcony overlooked a park and their short dead-end street contained new town-house buildings. The neighbourhood, close to a tram stop, was blessed with little car traffic. Jason simply loved both her fastidiousness in the toing and froing with housekeeping and the apparent ease in the way she despatched daily tasks. And his girth flourished from the delicacies in her diverse Asian cuisine.

Lucy also drew more confidence from her interactions with fellow female work colleagues at the information services firm where she had worked for some time. There, during after-work socials, she picked up relationship clues from her work mates' conversations about their male partners. These interactions also stimulated her fashion interests reflected in her more daring choices in outfits. Jason, a beneficiary of these transformations, felt that he was on pathway strewn with roses. And he was doubly proud of Lucy's portraiture skills which had commercial appeal. At the local Saturday market, she had a regular pitch where she managed to sell three to four portraits over the day.

Lucy's father remained a concern. Though he welcomed Jason and always showed love to his daughter, there was certainly an impression that he did not embrace the companion route she had taken. In Jason's company he was uneasy and conversations were punctuated with silence. This contrasted with his lively interactions with Bonnie and Don. Lucy hoped, over time, he would warm to Jason. She explained her father had strong conservative and traditional views on relationships and it was unlikely he would change.

He rarely visited their apartment with his wife, who, in her quiet way, adored Jason.

Up North Clare, Jack and daughter, Emma, well settled in the Redcliffe peninsula, revelled in the exploding opportunities of a Brisbane and a State on the move. Clare had joined the insurance industry and retrained as a contract assessor for property insurance claims. Working from home made it easy to support her daughter attending a local private school. An early decision meant that Emma was their only child.

Jack continued as chief executive of the Queensland operations of his firm. An unchallenging work environment and associated sedentary life programmed him for a bulky physique. Abundance of seafood, endless barbecues and relaxing lifestyle conspired to produce a hefty, loving husband. Their harmonious marriage never ceased to surprise Stella. Jack capitalised on Clare's continuing enthusiasm for matrimonial bonding and was able to make light of her withering frown when a disagreement arose.

The northern warmth and humidity, together with social life on the peninsula, encouraged even more flare in Clare's choice of clothing. Even with a fuller figure she was able to find dashing colours and drape styles which flattered her height and enhanced her willowy beauty. Jack noticed she continued to draw admiring looks at social gatherings. He could not believe how Clare had slipped easily into a gracious hostess role at social and work events. Her charm radiated and no doubt had some bearing on his management ratings by his firm.

Their social functions at home included locals, southern new arrivals, and work colleagues. Clare's developing expertise in social herding and corralling ensured that, at gatherings, there was seamless and unobtrusive intermixing, where strangers often found themselves becoming part of a network of new chums. And they noticed how she was always at ease. Stella, who witnessed some of this social prowess, could not believe the changes from the indifference and nonchalance of Homebush days.

Both Jack and Clare took care to be a-political amongst their neighbours. They saw how destructive the discussions of personal political positions were for relationships, particularly when amplified through social media. Friendships were destroyed as a result. They steered away from discussing local politics at all costs taking care also to avoid pointing out the virtues of life experienced in other parts of Australia. Many locals, despite the surge of cosmopolitan life, possessed a certain insularity and could be irritated when comparisons were explored.

Grandmother Stella enjoyed her times with Emma, and was regularly taken by her likeness of Emma to Clare. Emma had certainly inherited her lean genes. It was clear that Clare and Jack took parenting seriously. Emma, at home and at school, had the cheeriest and friendliness of dispositions, enjoyed company and easily accommodated the behaviour boundaries her parents had set. Importantly, Emma had good times with Fiona when visiting Stella for overnight stays.

The five-year anniversary of Fiona and Stella living together, in Fiona's late father's house, was quietly celebrated. Fiona had proposed they live together following her father's death but agreed not to exchange vows. Their romance had accelerated, following their exhibition week love tryst. They managed to take regular short holidays to exotic island resorts in the Pacific and their favourite Ubud getaway in Bali. The beguiling Fiona now matched Stella on romantic encounters.

There was no holding back from the reserved Fiona. Stella also found that the dimensions of love explored with Bonnie and Isabella seemed strangely tame compared with the unrelenting enthusiasm of the vigorous and awakening Fiona. The love genie had exploded out of the bottle and then some. A life together was assured.

Both had maintained exercise routines to keep fitness a priority. Apart from regular Pilates sessions they had a long active membership of a ladies' cycle group, which offered challenging rides into the hinterland of Brisbane. Stella served as President of the group for eight years.

The wiriness of Stella contrasted with the solid athleticism of Fiona. Greying hair had not eluded them, but they countered this with styling and subdued colouring. Out and about became their mantra for life. A successful business partnership had also evolved.

Through American contacts, Fiona had commenced an on-line business to sell supplementary diet products, initially through her pharmacy. It expanded so quickly that new premises were rented and Stella resigned her job to take on its management. Stella's new found entrepreneurial skill had tapped into new market segments, including health resorts, retirement villages and treatment clinics. Whilst the pharmacy business maintained its position, the supplement-supply operations provided a surprising surge in profits. Both the business and love partnerships flourished.

News between Sydney and Brisbane eventually faded. Bonnie and Stella retired. Their final journeys brought happiness and love and were rewarded by the joyful lives of Jason and Clare.

OBITUARY EXTRACT BONNIE
(PASSED 79 YEARS OLD)

.....she enjoyed the unstinting love and support from Don who was her devoted companion and mate. Their life was blessed with a wonderful mutual caring. Friends and relatives could not believe the depth of their seemingly impregnable bond. In her last years during her increasing frailty and decline from an incurable cancer, Don, her ever loving partner, was an unstoppable force, managing and coping with all the home-nursing demands.... Carmelita gave her special joy and pride. Carmelita's University work at nearby Glebe allowed regular visits. They were inseparable pals as they enjoyed visits to galleries and garden exhibitions. Delivering much joy to Bonnie was how well the relationship of Jason and Lucy had blossomed and matured. She was deeply gratified about their inseparability .... Bonnie's big heartedness and fun-spirited soul was always there for others to share, either at work in the garden centre, or with friends... Don's famous barbecues saw Bonnie as the ever-genial hostess. Guests were always bathed in her warmth and charm.... There were periods in her earlier life in Sydney when there were emotional setbacks and challenges but she managed to pivot away from them and to finally enjoy unconditional love from Don over the last 20 years.... Her fervour for life and enormous heart had delivered Bonnie rightful and deserved happiness in her retirement... She is memorialised by a beautiful fountain and garden in a small dedicated alcove at the garden centre, where she spent much of her working life

OBITUARY EXTRACT STELLA (PASSED 81 YEARS)

... Her family were deeply saddened that she would miss the wedding of her cherished granddaughter, Emma... Fiona, by her side when she collapsed and died on their daily walk, has been her constant loving partner after they wound up their business interests 12 years ago.... Stella, when in her mid-50s, moved to Brisbane where she enjoyed good fortune following some turmoil in her life in Sydney, her home town. Her Brisbane-based daughter Clare and her husband, Jack, saw Stella bloom in the long, loving relationship with Fiona, whom she met soon after arriving in Brisbane.... Her outstanding business acumen was on display in the successful dietary business she ran with Fiona. Both were widely respected for their organisational ability and industry ...They were constant visitors to Clare's home and shared the joy of Emma's successes at school and university. In later years, Stella often joined Clare on short trips abroad where their relationship deepened and flourished.... Never far from each other, Stella and Fiona were a handsome couple whom friends admired for the devotion and care they gave each other following their retirement... Stella's many years of contributions as President of the Cycle-Brisbane club and Queensland amateur cycling, were recognised by an OAM... In memory of Stella, Fiona has set up a financial trust to make an annual award and international travel scholarship to the top performing female cyclist in Queensland...

www.ingramcontent.com/pod-product-compliance
Lightning Source LLC
Chambersburg PA
CBHW061104100726
47911CB00012B/390